PAPERBACK JACK

Books by Loren D. Estleman

**AMOS WALKER
MYSTERIES**

Motor City Blue
Angel Eyes
The Midnight Man
The Glass Highway
Sugartown
Every Brilliant Eye
Lady Yesterday
Downriver
Silent Thunder
Sweet Women Lie
Never Street
The Witchfinder
The Hours of the Virgin
A Smile on the Face of the Tiger
Sinister Heights
*Poison Blonde**
*Retro**
*Nicotine Kiss**
*American Detective**
*The Left-Handed Dollar**
*Infernal Angels**
*Burning Midnight**
*Don't Look for Me**
*You Know Who Killed Me**
*The Sundown Speech**
*The Lioness Is the Hunter**
*Black and White Ball**
*When Old Midnight Comes
    Along**

*Cutthroat Dogs**
*Monkey in the Middle**

**VALENTINO,
FILM DETECTIVE**

*Frames**
*Alone**
*Alive!**
*Shoot**
*Brazen**
*Indigo**

DETROIT CRIME

Whiskey River
Motown
King of the Corner
Edsel
Stress
*Jitterbug**
*Thunder City**

PETER MACKLIN

Kill Zone
Roses Are Dead
Any Man's Death
*Something Borrowed,
    Something Black**
*Little Black Dress**

*Published by Tom Doherty Associates

PAPERBACK JACK

LOREN D. ESTLEMAN

A Tom Doherty Associates Book New York

PAPERBACK JACK

Copyright © 2022 by Loren D. Estleman

A Forge Book
Published by Tom Doherty Associates
120 Broadway
New York, NY 10271

www.tor-forge.com

Forge® is a registered trademark of Macmillan Publishing Group, LLC.

The Library of Congress Cataloging-in-Publication Data is available upon request.

ISBN 978-1-250-82731-9 (hardcover)
ISBN 978-1-250-82732-6 (ebook)

Our books may be purchased in bulk for promotional, educational, or business use. Please contact your local bookseller or the Macmillan Corporate and Premium Sales Department at 1-800-221-7945, extension 5442, or by email at MacmillanSpecialMarkets@macmillan.com.

First Edition: 2022

Printed in the United States of America

0 9 8 7 6 5 4 3 2 1

This book is dedicated to the memory of Donald Hamilton, Gordon D. Shirreffs, Richard Matheson, and Harlan Ellison, whose books found their largest readership during the Golden Age of the paperback, and whom I was privileged to call my friends; also to their colleagues, who along with them helped to create that distinctly American tradition: art from junk.

If it is art, it will offend before it is revered. There are calls for its destruction and then the bidding begins.

—E. L. Doctorow, *Homer & Langley*

PART ONE

1946
PENNY A WORD

CHAPTER
ONE

The Remington Streamliner portable was black, glossy, curved, with a sleek low profile like a Cadillac roadster. It had four rows of black-and-silver keys, but three keys were enameled in ruby red. One, the tabulator (largely useless except to accountants), was labeled SELF STARTER.

The typewriter—for that's all it was, despite the trimmings—compared to his old gray Royal standard like a spaceship parked next to a hay wagon. In a pawnshop window it was absurdly out of place, surrounded by egg-beaters and pocket watches, bouquets of fountain pens, a Chock full o'Nuts coffee can filled with wire-rimmed spectacles tangled inextricably like paper clips, a full set of the *World Book Encyclopedia* (outdated emphatically by events in Munich and Yalta). It looked proud and disdainful, a prince in exile.

And it spoke to him.

"My keys will never tangle or stick," it said. "I will never skip a space or type above or below the line. All I ask is a cleaning now and then, a little light oil, and I will serve you faithfully forever. Together we will change the face of literature."

Jacob tugged on the handle to the door of the shop. It wouldn't budge. A tin sign in the barred window told him to ring the bell. He pressed a brass button. There was a pause, then a buzz and a clunk, and he pulled the door open. That was something new in the world of retail. It belonged in a prison film.

The proprietor was an anachronism in green felt sleeve-protectors, black unbuttoned vest powdered with gray ash, and a green eyeshade that turned his long narrow face the color of a pickle. His red bow tie was so surrealistically crooked it might have been tied that way deliberately. He stood behind an old-fashioned wooden counter that reached to his sternum. The cardboard recruiting poster on a shelf behind him might have been merchandise, or it might have been stood up there by a previous owner and forgotten: The snarling German soldier wore a spiked helmet from two wars ago. The colors were faded and the corners curled inward.

"Yes-s?" A slight hissing at the end, as if the man had drawn in too much breath for just that one syllable and the rest had to escape.

"What are you asking for the typewriter in the window?"

The proprietor reached up to adjust a pair of glasses he wasn't wearing, squinting past the visitor's shoulder in the direction of an item he knew was there. "Fifty dollars."

Jacob goggled. "I wouldn't pay that for a brand-new machine!"

"Depression's over, mister. Cost of living's on the rise."

"I'll give you twenty-five." He could get a used Underwood from the Business Exchange for less; but it must be the Remington.

The man behind the counter registered funny-papers astonishment. Jacob was half surprised his eyeshade didn't fly off his head. "That's less than I gave the dame who brought it in."

"Do you know why she didn't redeem it?" He had a sudden doubt about the mechanics of the machine.

"It was her father's. Fergus Tunn, the poet? FBI tagged him for writing Nazi propaganda. They stuck him in a booby hatch upstate. She pawned it to keep him in straw to weave baskets. It was in all the papers."

There it was again, that accusatory coda: *It was in all the papers.* The uninformed were the second-class citizens of the postwar world. "When did this happen?"

"Last year sometime."

"Last year sometime I was in Brussels, waiting for my orders to ship home. If it made the papers there, it was in French. Or

Flemish, which no one speaks a hundred yards outside the borders. Thirty."

"Fifty's the price. Comes with a case, pebbled-black fabric with chromium latches. It's a quality item."

Jacob wished he'd worn his uniform and medals. They had a wizard effect; or had, before the parades on Fifth Avenue lost their novelty. His suit was the one he'd worn to basic training, and it was out of fashion even then, but it had fit. Now it hung loose around the belly and cinched tight at the shoulders. "Can't a veteran get a break?"

A tongue came off a tooth with a sharp snick. "Vets. Spoiled buggers."

"*Spoiled?*"

"Sure. All them free ham steaks and gasoline to burn while us Home Fronters had to hoard stamps to buy baloney and drive clear out to Coney Island for a little sun, which I think was rationed too. Now you want a deal just 'cause you wasn't smart enough to dodge the draft. I ask you."

"Just for that, ten, you son of a bitch!" Jacob scooped out his Army .45 and slammed it on the counter.

The muscles in the proprietor's face shut down. He groped under the counter and lifted a short-barreled revolver into line with Jacob's chest.

"This's New York, Joe. The *milk*man packs iron."

He put away the pistol. He'd packed it for muggers; he hadn't expected to need it indoors even in that neighborhood.

The revolver vanished. "Next time I call the cops. Four-flusher."

The buzzer let him out, blowing a raspberry.

Jacob drank six jiggers of Four Roses in a joint down the street called Ted's Last Chance. It was of a piece with its surroundings, plopped between a check-cashing place and a Salvation Army store that smelled like old gym socks: Dead fighters struck old-fashioned stances in flyblown frames behind the bar. The juke kept playing "I'll Never Smile Again." Sots blubbered in their Schlitz.

After Last Call, when the only lights burning in the pawnshop were the little Christmas bulbs at the back to discourage burglars, Jacob threw a brick through the window and ran away with the Remington under his arm. He almost tossed a sawbuck into the vacant spot, but he might as well have left a card. And the alarm was clanging at his heels.

He'd pulled a gun on a civilian and robbed a legitimate place of business. He was a fugitive.

His name was Jacob Heppleman. He was twenty-nine years old, unmarried but no virgin, and thanks to the war was in as good a physical condition as he'd ever been or was ever likely to be. He was a writer, or had been before Pearl. Although he'd written a good deal about the sort of person who threw bricks through windows and snatched what was on the other side, he'd always dismissed them as freaks of nature, career crooks or wretches driven by ignorance or bad company into a Life of Crime: Fellows with broken noses, who doubled all their negatives and ended their sentences with prepositions; plot devices. This was the first criminal act of his life. It left him mortified, as if he'd been caught masturbating by the rabbi.

But three blocks away, with no police whistles in pursuit, no sirens, no warning shots into the air—none of the tricks he employed on paper to goose up suspense—he slowed to a stroll, shifting the weight of the Remington under his other arm to rest its mate. He might have been taking home a legitimate purchase. *No, thanks, don't bother to wrap it. I don't have far to go.*

It was a fine fall evening, geese squawking in Central Park; no reason for them to map out the migration just yet. It made a man sanguine. Petty theft, what was that? It wasn't as if anything he'd fought for still applied.

Halfway home, he realized he'd left the carrying case behind.

CHAPTER TWO

It was funny he'd thought of the Business Exchange back in the pawnshop. That was where his life had begun.

He'd been twenty-one, on his own and out of work. On the way home from his final confrontation with the foreman, he'd stopped in a drugstore for a cup of coffee and the want ads, but the bright colors on the cover of a magazine called *Double-Barreled Detective* caught his eye and he bought it and read it at the counter.

The stuff was tripe. He didn't know much about gunshot wounds (not then), but he was sure that no man on earth could floor a mob of thugs in a dingy hotel room with just his fists and with a forty-five slug in his shoulder to boot. But he assumed someone had been paid for writing the scene. He didn't bother to go back and read the byline.

On the back page, among smudgy black-and-white illustrations advertising fertility pills and elevator shoes, he'd spotted a clip-art picture of a boxy typewriter and an order blank for a used machine from the International Business Exchange for as low as $26.95.

He'd gotten out his wallet and counted the bills inside. "How much, buddy?" he asked the man in the paper hat behind the counter.

"Dime for the cup of mud, dime for the magazine. Twenty cents, Rockefeller."

He had two tens, a five, and two singles in the wallet. From his pants pocket he counted out two dimes and a penny. $27.21. He smacked down the dimes and a penny tip for the Rockefeller crack. That left him with five cents bus fare and just enough for the machine.

That's how Jacob Heppleman became a writer.

His first story, "Before I Go into Shock," ran in the December 1938 issue of *Double-Barreled Detective*, entitled "A Punk with a Rod." He was paid twenty-five dollars for 2,500 words. It had taken him three months to write, two-finger fashion, on a stodgy Royal standard with a crooked *d*, and another month to hear back from the editor, but it returned almost a hundred percent on his investment—when the story appeared in print.

Not counting paper, ribbons, and postage. But the storefront accountant he consulted told him the expenses were tax deductible. He charged five bucks for the advice.

It was a joke; in school, had Jacob studied arithmetic more and English less, he'd be earning five bucks an hour instead of a penny a word. But it didn't take a Euclid to know that if you wrote twice as fast you'd make twice as much, and if you winnowed three months down to three days . . .

Well, it was still chump change. But it beat duking it out with some ape of a foreman for six-eighty a shift and kicking back four bits to the shop steward.

Had Sir Walter Scott started out this way? Likely not; but Walter hadn't anticipated the Great Depression.

By his twenty-third birthday, Jacob Heppleman had sold crime stories to *Double-Barreled Detective, Goon Squad, Third Degree,* and *Silk Sheets* (a racy-thriller magazine, with a woman on the cover falling out of her lingerie; he was afraid to be seen admiring it in the drugstore), and westerns to *Six-Gun Sagas, Warbonnet, Tin Star, Rawhide Riders,* and *Badlands.* When he got tired of powwows and saloons he shifted gears, but after "Amazon Maidens of the Moon" had made the rounds of *Orbit, Constellation, Astounding Science Fiction,* and *Tales From Outer Space,* and come back with dog ears and coffee rings, he chucked it.

"Custer's Ghost" was his last oater; everyone was either a paleface or a sidewinder, and he kept losing track of where the hero left his horse. At that point his rent was paid up and he had pork chops in the icebox, so he cranked in a sheet of yellow paper and spent a month on *Chinese Checkers,* about skullduggery in Chinatown, a place he'd visited only once, and got sick on bad chow mein. It ran 60,000 words and was serialized in five issues of *Double-Barreled Detective.* He'd written his first novel.

It caught the attention of a literary agent, who spent twenty minutes on the phone explaining why he needed representation. Finally: "Look, you can be a pulp writer all your life or you can play with the big boys. I'm talking Steinbeck. Hemingway. That dame, she wrote about deer?"

"Marjorie Kinnan Rawlings. *The Yearling.*" He almost never read in his own field anymore. "You're serious?"

"The *Hindenburg,* that was serious. I'm talking im-fucking-mortality."

He was impressed: It was the first time he'd heard anyone split a word in order to insert an obscenity. He agreed to hire the agent for a ten percent commission.

After three rejections, the agent, Ira Winderspear, placed *Chinese Checkers* with The Thornberry Press, an old Boston concern, recently inherited by the great-grandson of the founder, and a fan of detective fiction. Many months of revisions and rewrites followed: There were too many blackjacks, the publisher said, too many riddled bodies falling through doorways. On the final stroke of the last draft, the Business Exchange machine broke, sending the crooked *d* zinging past his left ear.

The book appeared in November 1941, bound in cloth with yellow-and-black Deco on the dust jacket. Sales were modest, but it was favorably reviewed in *Literary Digest.*

Jacob never saw the review. He was in New Jersey when that issue came out, in basic training at Fort Dix. Pearl Harbor was burning and the Second World War was on.

CHAPTER
THREE

The war was over: but the battle with his conscience had just begun.

The first time he sat at the Remington, a wave of guilt swept over him. He'd never so much as stolen gum from the five-and-dime. Then he thought of the pawnshop owner, what he'd said about the men who'd fought for his right to own anything, and he was serene for the moment.

But he promised himself to go back and square things. It would be galling; but then that was something else he'd fought for, the good and just laws that protected everyone.

Which was laying it on thick. It was interesting what committing a crime did for one's self-righteousness.

The machine worked fine. He was clumsy at first; he hadn't typed a line in almost five years, and the keystroke was longer than the Royal's. When he'd warmed up enough to work at his old speed, the keys jammed and he had to separate them by hand. (The Streamliner had fibbed about that; but then it was just trying to make the sale.)

His fear of writer's block, that maybe he'd left whatever talent he had in some bombed-out farmhouse in Belgium, vanished by the time the bell rang at the end of page one. *They waded through wheat waist-high, each of them thinking of the same things: the misty rain soaking their wool uniforms, the way the drops beaded on the barrels of their BARs, the musty smell of wet grain, the hissing sound the spikes made against their pants legs as they walked, the misery of sodden socks: everything but what their drill sergeants had drummed into them in Basic: "Krauts, Krauts, Krauts, morning, noon, and night. You eat Krauts, you crap Krauts, you fuck Krauts in your dreams."*

And then they saw their first one. . . .

They'd been with him since Antwerp, those words, in that order. He'd thought of making notes, but it was his fate to forget a thing the moment he wrote it down. If he lost the notes—which was likely; sooner or later everything got lost on the march—he would never get the words back. And so he'd repeated them, in his head and aloud, in the shower, when he was shaving, when he laced up his boots, whenever he wasn't actually walking into harm's way. The other guys in the outfit called him Charlie McCarthy, Edgar Bergen's dummy, "on account of Heppleheimer's always talking, but he don't know what he's saying."

Which was when he'd determined to keep his mouth shut. If he'd feared anything more than death or the loss of a limb, it was that one of his eavesdroppers would be invalided home and write the damn book before he could.

By the time he became accustomed to waking up on his own schedule, with some savings left in the bank, he had three solid chapters and the only outline he'd ever written. He found his old address book and called Winderspear, hoping the number was still in service.

"Hey, hey!" That same gusty greeting in the burring voice marinated in Brooklyn, as if they'd spoken yesterday, with no war in between. The man was a permanence, like the skyscraper where he worked. "Johnny came home. How's the hero? Bring back any Jap souvenirs?"

"Wrong theater, Ira. When can I see you?"

"Anytime, kid. My door's always open to clients and vets."

The door was framed in oak, IBW LITERARY AGENCY painted on the frosted glass, fifteen floors up in the Chrysler Building. It opened directly into Winderspear's office, oak also, the desk and chairs and file cabinets and three paneled walls, the fourth mostly window looking out on New York City as it appeared on postcards, golden under a cloudless blue sky. Even the man sitting at the desk behind stacks of manuscripts looked like an oak blasted by lightning, his face and bald head gnarled and brown.

"Hey, hey! Fit as a fiddle and ready for work. Looks like you grew six inches over there. In-fucking-credible."

"Hello, Ira. I see you're still too cheap to hire a secretary." He felt himself grinning. It was as if he'd never left. It might have been the same pile on the desk.

"I thought about it a couple times, but they were all busy being Rosie the Riveter, building planes and shit. Anyway, what's the point?" The word rhymed with *burnt*. "They'd slide right off my lap." He patted his paunch where his vest wouldn't close and got up to extend a hand. Withered he might have appeared, but his grip could crush gravel. "Jesus, you look like Randolph Scott. I bet the *Fräuleins* wet their pants every time you liberated a town."

"*Mademoiselles*, you mean. I never got to Germany."

"French ass; even better. At ease, soldier." He sat.

Jacob nestled himself into yet more oak, polished by hundreds of buttocks, and laid the scuffed leather briefcase in his lap.

Winderspear saw it. "Been working, good. I was afraid you gave me the brush-off. I expected you a week after V-J Day."

"V-E Day, for me; but there was talk of shipping us to the Pacific. The marines were hard up for help. After Truman dropped the pill on Hiro-whatever and my discharge came through, I wintered in Paris: Been back six months. Here's what took so long." He drew forth the outline and three chapters and put them in the agent's hands.

Winderspear hooked on his glasses and read rapidly. That was another thing that hadn't changed. The first time Jacob saw it, he thought he couldn't be taking it all in; then he'd pointed out everything that was wrong in detail.

This time, though, he hesitated, which wasn't like the Ira he remembered. He took off the glasses, sighed, tapped the top page with an earpiece, sat back, curled his gnarled fingers over the arms of his swivel, where they appeared to have been carved from the same wood.

"Did I dangle a participle?" Jacob smiled, a ghost of his greeting grin. Suddenly he felt the way he did every time his unit was called up to the front, the same old butterflies in the stomach.

"Hell, no. It's good. You couldn't write a bad line in a hurricane, that was never a problem. You see these?" He lifted a hand and aimed it at the papers in front of him. "Pick one up and read it. Any one, doesn't matter. They're all the war. Every day a fresh load comes in over the transom. You'd think there'd be one G.I. didn't go over there Willie Gillis and come back Ernie Pyle."

"So what? How many private eye stories did you place before the war?"

"That was different. Public couldn't get enough of those. They've had five years of blood and guts till they're green in the face: army green. If Audie Murphy came through that door right now with his memoirs under his arm, I'd have to turn him away."

"Okay, so no regular publisher. But if we serialize—"

"Yeah, but where?"

"Where? *Combat Action. Guts and Glory. Battlefield.*"

"They all went south with Hitler's brains. And it's not just the war rags. Whole pulp market's kaput. First it was the wartime paper shortage—seen *The Creeper* lately, *Racket Busters*? Gone digest size. Cut the material they buy in half. Then they just stopped selling. Thirty years—hell, *eighty*, counting Buffalo Bill yarns—up in smoke." He blew an invisible smoke ring. "Want to write for the comic books? That's where the market is now."

"Comic books are for kids."

"We'll be up to our asses in kids just as soon as all those Johnnies finish putting their Class-As in mothballs and start banging the old lady. Wait till television gets going. It's not much now, old movies and boxing, but the sets are outselling toasters five to one, and it isn't toast that's in trouble. Wouldn't surprise me if the schools stop teaching the little bastards to read."

"When Edison invented the phonograph they said it was the end of live orchestras. Been to the Philharmonic lately?"

"Phonograph records cost dough. You have to go on buying them or you'll flip your lid listening to Kay Kyser all day long. Television programs are free, and they just keep coming, even when you're sleeping, like a hard-on. Ten cents for a pulp? Might as well be ten bucks."

Jacob felt the abyss at his feet. He sat back to keep from falling in.

Winderspear opened a gnarled fist in a gesture of dismissal. "Cheer up, kid. There's a cloud around every silver lining." He rolled his chair back far enough to open the top drawer of his desk without bumping his belly. "I know you've seen these. The government put 'em in with the K rations, free from the publishers." He slid something down an aisle between papers.

It was a slim book about the size of a cigarette case, bound in paper with page-ends dyed red and a glossy cover, varnished and sealed in laminate. In the foreground stood a man with his back half-turned away, watching an overripe blonde undressing in the background. She was clearly the focus of the picture, painted in rich oils: blood reds, cerecloth blacks, and school bus yellows. The title, *Half-Past Midnight*, was in white sanserif letters, as was the smaller-type byline, Clifton Eldridge.

"I got Armed Services editions along with every other dog-face," Jacob said. "I know what they look like: cheap and tawdry. I read this book before the war, in cloth. I don't remember any women undressing in front of men in it."

"Not the point. How many copies you figure sold?"

"It's been around for years. Ten or twenty thousand."

"This one sold just under a million."

"Bullshit."

"Glad to see you expanded your vocabulary abroad. I know Eldridge's agent; well, Eldridge croaked in 'forty, so he represents the widow. She bought a house in Florida last winter. Paid cash. I'm telling you, these two-bit editions fly off the racks."

"You think you can sell *That Mad Game* to this outfit?"

"What mad game?"

"You just read it! It's from Swift: 'That mad game the world so loves to play.'"

"Yeah. I never look at titles. Waste of time. Publishers are always changing 'em. No, I just got through telling you war books are a drug on the market. Here." He reached inside the drawer again, pushed another book after the first, only this time he covered it with his hand.

Jacob felt the butterflies again.

Winderspear looked up at him from under his burled-oak brow. "This is a mock-up. Blank inside. The publisher wanted you to see how it'll look when it's finished."

The painting might have been by the same artist, using the same splashy color scheme as *Half-Past Midnight*. This time the woman was Asian, with short, blue-black hair in bangs, dressed in a silk kimono open almost to her nipples. What appeared to be the same man, stripped to the waist and tied to a chair, watched with a snarling expression as the woman advanced on him holding a stiletto with a blade as thin and sharp as a needle. *Chinese Checkers.* The title of Jacob's novel. There was no byline.

"I swung the deal while you were gone. It's not kosher, but I didn't know how to reach you and the publisher was hot to trot. You know how often that doesn't happen. Jack, all I'm asking is don't blow your top till you hear me out."

"My name is Jacob."

"Not anymore."

CHAPTER FOUR

"What's the matter with Jacob Heppleman?"

"Guess."

"*Ira Winderspear* thinks my name's too Jewish?"

"It's not my name on the cover. Look, everyone knows what you did over there, liberating the camps."

"Those were in Poland. I never got that far."

"I mean you brave guys. There are people kvetching that we went to war just for the Jews. They're punks, but their two bits spend the same as everyone else's. Let things settle a couple years, then you can put everything back in print: *Jacob Heppleman*, thirty-six-point type: *writing as Jack Holly*, eighteen. Jack Holly, a swashbuckler of a name. Errol Flynn wishes he had it."

"It sounds like a card sharp. Who thought of it?"

"I came up with Jack. Holly was Robin Elk's."

"He could use a new name himself. Who is he?"

"Elk. You know, like the moose. He's the money." Winderspear tapped the upper left corner of the mock-up.

Jacob looked at an image the size of his thumbnail, a caricature of a cherubic blue demon with button horns, rocket-trail eyebrows, a naughty grin, and a dished-in nose like the swoop of a roller-coaster track. "Blue Devil Books," he read. "Never heard of it."

"It's new. Elk wants to publish new work in cheap editions: Paperback originals, he calls 'em. Nobody's ever done that. It's less of a gamble to issue a book with a publishing history by an established author. Personally I think he'll lose his shirt, but meantime you'll get dough up front to stake you till you get your toe back in."

"What happened to those million-copy sales?"

"I won't jack you around, kid. The cancer didn't stop with the pulps. Another Eldridge, *Harbor Girl*, didn't sell through. Maybe the vets are too busy buying houses in the suburbs and going to college on the G.I. Bill to read for pleasure. Blue Devil's looking to cut its costs by developing its own authors: Deal out the middle man, go short up front, and split the royalties fifty-fifty. Maybe he's onto something, I don't know. It's a different world since you went away. Nobody's got a handle on it just yet." He held out *That Mad Game*. "Stick this in a drawer till the next war. Write another *Chinese Checkers*."

Jacob left him hanging while he turned over the mock-up and read the copy on the back. The top line was printed in red, in type twice as large as the rest in black:

"I HUNGER FOR A WHITE MAN!"

Paul Matson came to Chinatown looking for a good time. The times found him, but they weren't good; in fact, they were wicked. He had barely set foot in Ah Lo Wing's Garden of Celestial Delights when sinuous, inscrutable Lee Sin pounced from the shadows like a panther from the Far East, with lust in her heart and evil on her mind.

"I hunger for a white man," she purred in Matson's ear. "Come, and I will show you the ancient Oriental ways of love."

He was suddenly violently ill; partly from the betrayal, as much from the unexpected exposure to the blind racism of youth, before experience had opened his eyes. His face was hot. "Nix. I didn't fight a war to land back where I started."

"War's over, kid. You remember those ads for trusses and hemorrhoid cream? Gap in the action. Sure, they paid the bills. All you boys paid the bills. But the public doesn't buy toothpaste to read the label on the back. The war, it was a gap: a time-out, like in football. You turn the page, get back to the game where it left off."

"Gee, I missed that in the recruiting posters. JOIN THE ARMY, BE A GAP."

"What do you think people want, after all those stories of bayonetings and machine-gun massacres? It's the flag-waving they got tired of. So you give 'em what they want, only without the brass bands. Brother, you thought the pulps were bloody, but you ain't seen nothing yet."

A siren wailed fifteen floors down, stopping as abruptly as it had started, as if the prowlie was testing it. A Michigan farm boy who'd shaken loose the dirt as soon as he had bus fare, Jacob had never gotten over how New York racket managed to penetrate the ritziest buildings.

"Last time I looked at my contract with Thornberry, it said I had to approve subsidiary offers. Back then it meant moving pictures and radio, but I'm sure it covers this. What'd you do, forge my signature?"

"I resent that. I traced it from the original contract."

He knew his agent was a millionaire: His office rent was more than the government had spent on Jacob's bed and board from boot camp on. He'd survived a Depression and a war and from the look of his belly hadn't missed a meal at Sardi's or 21 since before the Blitz. He was a man of means and power. So Jacob chose his words carefully.

"You're fired, Ira."

Winderspear blinked. His eyes were the only animated feature in that petrified-wood face. "You don't want to do that. I'm a rabbit's foot. Everyone who's ever fired me wound up in Dutch, starting with Arnold Rothstein when I ran liquor for him in Jersey; clients were hard to come by, I had to make ends meet. Six weeks after he canned me, somebody put a slug in him in the Park Central Hotel."

"You're threatening me. I don't believe it. What are you, some kind of gangster?"

"Christ, *I* didn't shoot him. But if he kept me on, who knows?

The slob might've missed. I got more stories, but that's your racket, not mine. I just sell 'em."

"I'll risk it. And if I see so much as one copy of that piece of shit in a drugstore or bus station, I'll tell Robin Elk what you did. If he's any kind of businessman he'll have you arrested for fraud." He got up.

"I was looking after your interests. How was I to know you got religion over there? The guy that wrote this book, him I could reason with. He'd've jumped all over this deal."

"He grew up."

"Easy, Jack. Don't go off half-cocked."

"Why not? That's how I came in. And don't call me Jack!" He opened the door.

"What are you going to do?"

"Go back to school, what else? I can't afford a house in the suburbs." He slammed it.

CHAPTER FIVE

He worked for a Manhattan advertising agency, Barlow, O'Keefe, Brogan, & Associates, for a week. It had four floors in a bank building on Madison Avenue, a glossy skyscraper that resembled a buzz-bomb stood on end. A giant four-color poster of a loaf of bread shaped like a sleek locomotive greeted him when he stepped off the elevator, wind lines streaming along its sides: Sunrise Bakeries was the account that had put the firm on the map.

The offices were glass fishbowls and you signed a time sheet instead of punching in, but apart from the show it was the same kind of dirty-neck job he'd traded for a typewriter all those years ago; the foremen just wore Arrow collars. The pace reminded him of D-Day, except only the enemy was armed. When the copy he'd submitted for the Best Buddy Dog Food account came flying out the Creative Director's door folded into a paper plane, he quit.

After pounding the pavement for three weeks, he sat down with the city editor of *The Greenwich Clock,* a daily paper that had started out catering to the Bohemian artistic community, then had gone head-to-head with the tabloids, running headlines like WIFE SLAYS HUSBAND, MISTRESS, SELF, just before the stock market crashed and readers bought copies only to line their worn-out shoes.

By that time there was no going back; the painters, hoofers, and would-be Eugene O'Neills who used to subscribe were operating forklifts. Somehow the newspaper hung on, crowded into one floor of a former glove factory in SoHo with a Chinese restaurant at ground level. Every square inch smelled of frying oil and when Jacob handed the editor his application, grease from the staircase banister left transparent fingerprints on the sheet.

The editor, Sam Rosetti, might have modeled for a comical illustration in *Paper Tigers,* a journalist-themed pulp: His hairline started two fingers above his bushy brows, the tracks of the comb as visible as tread marks in tar, grew back and down inside his collar, getting steadily blacker and more coarse until it sprang from his rolled-up sleeves like uncoiled wire. The dead cigar in the corner of his mouth was just something to hold the place for the next. He spread the sheet on his filthy blotter and shoveled fried rice from a cardboard container into his mouth as he read. He was clumsy with chopsticks: When he finished, the application looked like a used placemat.

"When can you start?"

"Today." Jacob was surprised into an unseemly show of eagerness.

"'Kay. There's your desk. You'll have to clean it out. Keep what you can use, throw out the rest. Our last rewrite man croaked himself on wood alcohol last month."

"That's terrible."

"No shit. I had December in the pool. It don't say here you have newspaper experience, but it looks like you can string together a sentence, which is more than I can say for the jerk you're replacing, rest his soul." Rosetti crossed himself with his chopsticks. "Anyway, I'm sick of filling in. You know the job?"

"I think I can guess."

"Guessing's for radio. You wait for the phone to ring, you take down notes, you put 'em in English, and you get 'em in on deadline. *Plain* English, Shakespeare; we don't circulate on Park Avenue. Think you can handle that?"

He said yes. He'd hoped for a byline, but then he didn't plan to make journalism a career. His rent was ten days past due and he was sitting on his last twenty dollars like eggs in a nest, eating in automats and walking fifty blocks at a stretch to avoid paying bus fare.

The pulp picture wasn't quite as dismal as Winderspear had painted it—there were still plenty of titles on the stands, bright red and yellow as always, like ketchup and mustard containers in a railcar diner—but the heady days of editors buying stories hand over fist were no more. *Double-Barreled Detective* was gambling only on proven best-sellers from its glory days, *Goon Squad* was gone, *Third Degree* had shrunken to half its former size and was bought up into 1947 (if it lasted that long); inquiries around town confirmed that. The racy magazines, *Silk Sheets, Sultry Stories, Gams and Guns,* and *Muff Pistols* (Good God!) had, in their desperation to attract the lowest common denominator, sunk to pornographic depths that practically invited postal inspectors to seize them at the loading docks. The covers still walked the tightrope between tasteless and trial-by-jury, but the pen-and-ink drawings inside would make Mae West blush. Too bad, because they paid three times better than the others; but just the thought of writing such dreck made him want to take a bath.

The war pulps were gone, or as good as. *Daredevils and Dog-faces* and *Trench Tales* were still there, but they'd gone monthly, and the material seemed worn out even to him, who'd lived it. He doubted they'd last out the year.

There was a disturbing incursion of women's confession magazines—*My Secret Sin, Forbidden Romance, Broken Vows*—spilling out their litany of overripe confessions (i.e., female fantasies, or what the men who wrote them under names like Molly Ann Thompson and Susan Marie Klein assumed them to be), and shabby true detective rags with grainy photographic covers and real-life rape-and-slash stories catalogued up front, like a menu taped in the window of a doubtful eatery. And among them their bastard children, "tell-all" exposé rags with movie stars and lounge singers caught in unflattering moments by the glare of flashguns. By and large their contents were written by a handful of staffers under a variety of pseudonyms or assembled from newspaper clippings by anonymous file clerks. A daily diet of newsreels from the front had stripped away the last Edwardian vestiges of privacy and discretion.

And there were comic books: On the covers a flock of professional wrestlers dressed in capes and swimwear, leaping and soaring and beating up thugs, a menagerie of cartoon animals, a conga line of rotting zombies. Nothing that hadn't already been done by Uncle Remus, Edgar Allan Poe, Bulldog Drummond, and Tom Swift, this time drawn by crude artists with speech balloons (quote: "What the—?"). But Winderspear had been wrong about threats from that quarter. Children outgrew childish things.

His workday at the *Clock* started before dawn and he never got home before dark. Six days a week, the sun was a leaden rumor sliding through greasy glass. He ate lunch at his desk, but memories of spoiled chow mein—and *Chinese Checkers*—kept him from ordering from downstairs. A boy in a white coat and a paper hat brought him drugstore sandwiches and he washed them down with coffee from the vending machine in the hallway. The vendor seemed to be dumping what remained of the swill that had passed for the real thing during rationing, but at least it was hot, and the scalding stuff helped kill the taste of liverwurst.

The job was stimulating at first. The thunder of typewriters, the constant ringing of telephones, copy boys bustling about, snatching copy and dodging crumpled cardboard coffee cups launched at their heads—the eternal push to scoop the competition; *The Greenwich Clock* was uncut adrenaline. He saw himself as a fixture in *The Front Page*, drinking from a flask and spouting cynicisms.

The first story that came his way, rapped into his ear in the breathless tenor of a reporter on the scene, was a fire in a school for the underprivileged, with a Puerto Rican janitor thought to be trapped on the top floor. He took it all down in his personal shorthand. His rewrite passed muster with Rosetti, after he'd made slashing cuts with a fat blue pencil in one hand, chopsticks in the other. There was a deadline breathing hot down his hairy neck, so the refinements were minimal. Jacob had the satisfaction of proofing his own spare prose in galleys within the hour, fresh from the Linotype.

The janitor turned out to be okay, having deserted his post for an evening with the school nurse. Jacob despised himself for being disappointed.

He made no friends. The other reporters took coffee breaks that stretched into four hours in a bar called The Scribblers' Lounge, but they didn't invite him, and he couldn't have joined them if they had, chained as he was to the candlestick phone on his desk. The only one he'd have liked to ask him along was the sob sister, a hard-faced blonde with a nice figure who churned out tearjerkers about battered wives and runaway children; but she drifted past his desk without a glance in his direction. He wasn't attracted to her, especially, but after more than a year back in the States he missed sex.

But the stories couldn't all be about fires, or beat cops delivering babies, or Zoot Suiters brawling in the Bowery. He wrote up wedding ceremonies for the Society section, quiana lace and baby's-breath bouquets (a revolting name, upon consideration) and rapped out captions for pictures of couples celebrating golden wedding anniversaries, the snowy-haired former brides radiant and the rumpled erstwhile grooms looking like blessed death.

So this was postwar prosperity.

For sanity's sake he often read the want ads over lunch. One particularly soul-destroying day, he found a listing for a creative writing class being taught in a public school building on Twenty-Second Street. He dialed the number on an impulse. He'd been a professional writer for four years, allowing for his service and not counting two months with *The Greenwich Clock*. Maybe it was time he learned to be an amateur.

CHAPTER SIX

P.S. 187, a square brick building constructed on a wooden frame, looked like a fire station. Room 3-C belonged to every schoolhouse in North America. The cloakroom smelled of sour wool and rubber galoshes, and chalk and graphite salted every surface beyond, the first night, Jacob decided to spare his corduroy sportcoat and come to class from then on in flannel and denim. Drycleaning rates had gone up along with everything else.

The night-school crowd had to sit sideways at desk-and-chair sets designed for fifth-graders. A smudged geography lesson on the blackboard said the annual mean precipitation rate in the Andes was thirty to forty inches.

The instructor's name was Tharp. He was a balding man in his forties who for some reason wore a varsity jacket from a high school in Buffalo and sneakers that squeaked on the linoleum floor; the noise was like an ice pick in the brain. The course description said he was a published poet. He lectured on *theme* in a voice that droned when it was audible at all. His listeners coughed and squirmed in their hard small seats and sneaked glances at the big electric clock mounted above a bulletin board shingled with crayon drawings of turkeys and pilgrims.

Jacob gave up taking notes. He'd never understood *theme* and never would. If he'd mentioned the subject to any of his editors, they'd have stared as if he'd just stepped off an alien spaceship on the cover of *Astounding Science Fiction*. "Theme, fuck's that? Plot is God, kid." (Every writer was *kid* to editors and agents, even if he had white hair and an ear trumpet.) "When the story bogs down, shoot somebody."

The second night, he was asked to diagram a sentence. He understood syntax. He didn't know a second predicate from First Communion, but he knew where to place the active verb in a sentence, even if he couldn't explain why. But Tharp insisted his students apply rules to the English language that were better suited to math. When Jacob turned in his worksheet, it came back with a big red *D-*.

"Son of a bitch." He stared at the grade.

"He is, isn't he?"

He jumped. The woman seated across the aisle was leaning his way, an arm flung across the back of her chair, and had spoken low, behind the instructor's retreating back. Jacob had noticed her before. She was about his age, pleasant-looking, with her red hair in a shoulder bob and one of those suits that made women look like Charles Atlas. This one had nice legs where her skirt caught them at mid-calf. She hadn't paid him any attention until now, so he'd dismissed her as just another frustrated former defense worker done out of a job by a returning serviceman.

He was abashed. "Excuse my French. In high school I never scored lower than a *B* in Composition."

"Tharp would say that's the theme of today's story."

"This isn't discussion time, people." Tharp had come to the end of her row and turned to scowl at the pair.

"My fault, sorry," Jacob said.

"If I were you, Mr. Heppleman, I'd save my energy for concentration. You're getting a free ride, courtesy of the G.I. Bill. You should show your gratitude to the taxpayers by buckling down."

The woman spoke up. "Pardon me, Mr. Tharp. What branch of the military did you say you served in?"

The man's pasteboard face blossomed high on the cheeks. "I have an inner-ear condition, Miss Curry. I did my bit in the Civil Defense." He laid the sheet on her desk and moved on.

She glanced at the sheet, turned it over. "Shit."

"What'd he do to you?" Jacob was mildly shocked by her

language. Something had happened to femininity while he was away.

"Me? Nothing. I've had my fill of these four-effers looking down on veterans because they weren't smart enough to beat the system like them."

"I meant what grade did he give you?"

"Does it matter? I'm just here to learn how to write a decent letter. Secretarial work's all there is now."

He grinned. "Aced it, didn't you?"

"Not quite." She tapped a row of scarlet-painted nails on the sheet, then smiled and turned it over. She had a crooked smile.

He looked. "*B*-plus. What are you, a math whiz?"

"Well, don't say it like it's a criminal record."

He cleared his throat. "Sorry. I never learned to add, so I wrote for pennies."

"You're a professional writer? What have you written? Would I know it?"

The instructor chose that moment to address the class. Jacob was grateful for the timing.

"Going over your worksheets, I see some potential, some faint hope, and some despair for the race. This is an adult class, so I assume you all know where you belong in that scenario. During the next four weeks, we'll be discussing characterization, motivation, mechanics, and plot development. At the end of that time, I'll ask each of you to write a complete short story—I place the emphasis on *short*: By which I mean longer than two hundred words on how you spent your summer vacation, but not as long as *Forever Amber*; which on second thought would have spared the world a great deal of agony had it restricted itself to two hundred words. My time, judging by some of these exercises in construction"—Jacob swore he looked directly at him—"is a commodity I value more than some of you do yours. When I've read your contributions to culture, I'll be in a position to say whether there's hope for you or if you're better suited to writing jingles for Burma-Shave."

Jacob hoisted his briefcase and headed for the door. He hoped he gave Miss Curry the impression he was late for some appointment, not that he was ducking the subject of his body of work. ("No kidding, you're *that* Jacob Heppleman? The author of 'A Punk with a Rod'? I had no idea. Could I prevail upon you to autograph my copy of *Double-Barreled Detective*? Preferably in my apartment?")

Right.

He went back to the *Clock*, rolled a sheet into the cranky Underwood on his desk—and began his first short story in nearly six years:

> The Remington Streamliner portable was black,
> glossy, curved, with a sleek low profile like a Cadillac
> roadster....

It was automatic writing, as if the spirit of Fergus Tunn, the mad poet, haunted his old machine. A down-at-heels scribe, unable to afford a typewriter, steals one from a shop. Terrified of discovery, he tries to turn himself in to end the agony, only to learn that the theft was never reported, and therefore officially no crime has been committed. Just when he decides to put the past behind him and become a productive member of the literary establishment, he's arrested for the shop owner's murder, which took place later, and of which he's innocent. "The Typewriter" came in at 3,500 words and required little revising. It was as close to perfect as he'd ever come.

"*F?*"

"*Very* good, Mr. Heppleman. An understanding of the alphabet is the first sign you've shown of real literacy."

He'd lingered at the teacher's Noah's-Ark desk until the rest of the class had filed out, holding the rolled typescript of his story crushed in his fist. Tharp had circled the failing mark in still more scarlet, as if to vent dissatisfaction with the finite nature of the grading process. Had there been a *G,* the circle suggested, he'd have put it to use. The instructor stood, putting papers in a tattered leather portfolio and tying the strings.

"What's wrong with the story?" Jacob asked.

"Nothing, to the ill-read. It's a competent work of plagiarism."

"Plagiarism! I—" He stopped himself before confessing the story was based on experience.

"Victor Hugo and O. Henry would bear me out. It begins as *Les Misérables* and ends as 'The Cop and the Anthem.' I'm not incensed so much by the theft as by the assumption I'm unaware of the source material."

"Listen, Tharp, I'm a professional. I've got more ideas than I know what to do with. I've got no reason—"

"Yes, I read your biography on the enrollment form. The rags who published you couldn't have existed in Hugo's day or O. Henry's. It's a sad fact of universal literacy that the public's taste in reading has fallen so far. But to be charitable, let's assume your assault on intellectual property was an unconscious act. If you can write a new story—emphasis on *new*—and turn it in Tuesday, I'll give it a passing grade—if I like it—and we'll pretend this little slip never happened. This is a very good deal I'm offering; a veteran's benefit, let's say."

Jacob said, "I have a counter-offer."

———

Sucking his skinned knuckles, he almost bumped into the redhead in the hallway. They'd hardly spoken since the second day of class. Her eyebrows were raised. "What was *that*?" She crushed out her cigarette against the frame of the open window at the end by the stairs. "Was someone moving furniture?"

"That was the sound of me dropping out of school. Let's get a cup of coffee."

"Whoa, mister. Wartime speed limits are still in effect."

"I've stayed under them so far. I've asked you out for coffee the last four Tuesdays and Thursdays, and you've had somewhere to be every time. You don't seem to be in a hurry tonight."

"If you think I was waiting for you—"

"I need your answer, Miss Curry. When Tharp comes around, I may be wanted for assault and battery."

She smiled and hoisted the strap of her handbag higher on one padded shoulder. "Call me Ellen."

CHAPTER SEVEN

"Can I read your story?"

Jacob's tone took on a droning quality. "I assume you *can*, Miss Curry, ours being a nation of compulsory education. Whether you *may* is the point at issue."

She shuddered. "Golly, don't do that again. You sound too much like him."

"Be my guest. The *F* is for 'fine.'" Not bothering to open his briefcase, he'd folded the crumpled pages into a clumsy square and thrust it in a jeans pocket. Now he spread it out on the table between them.

They were in a booth at Woolworth's, across the aisle from the gleaming counter. The store was observing Christmas hours; the buzz of customer conversation mingled with Perry Como's crooning on the loudspeaker. Jacob drank from his cup and watched her read, one elbow on the table and the cigarette in her hand pointed toward the ceiling. She'd eaten half a chicken-salad sandwich and taken a refill on her coffee.

She read briskly, but she wasn't just skimming. Once she paged back to look at something again, then continued without pausing. When she came to the end she drummed the pages together and returned them. Smiled.

"That bad?" He refolded and stuffed them back inside his pocket.

"It's good. I like your hero. He knows he did wrong, but he doesn't get all weepy and hand-wringy over it. Frankly, that was the problem I had with Hugo. I've never read O. Henry, so I can't say anything about that."

"So you agree with Tharp."

"Gosh, no. I'd never have made the connection if you hadn't told me what he said. How many plots are there in the world, really?"

"Six. *Snow White, Cinderella, Goldilocks and the Three*—"

"I get you. No need to go on."

"Good. I can't think of the others."

"All those stories have heroines, not heroes."

"Tharp would just say I have trouble writing women."

"Did you really knock him out?"

"Silly, but not out. A man isn't as easy to KO as you see in pictures. I learned that at Fort Dix. I'm afraid to look at my old stuff. I put more guys to sleep with one punch than Joe Louis, and that was just in one story."

"I'd like to read your old stuff."

"Good luck. I left a trunk with my landlord. He sold the building while I was overseas and everything in it. You won't find them at the library." He blew on his cup, although it had stopped steaming ten minutes ago. "May I read yours?"

"I don't have any old stuff."

"Stop stalling, sister," he growled.

She laughed. The counterman looked up from his polish rag. "Did you really write like that?"

"I had to. Think the black market's risky? Try smuggling good dialogue past the editors at *Goon Squad*."

"*Goon Squad*, really?"

"Don't be a snob. Its sister publication was *The Cultural Quarterly*, which it outsold ten to one. The story, lady." He extended his palm, wiggling his fingers.

She opened her handbag and took out a sheaf of pages bound with a paper clip. He reached for it. She drew it back. "Promise you won't be kind."

"Cross my heart." He did.

She let him take it. He looked at the grade. "*A*-minus."

"Tharp asked me out a couple of times. He thinks he can pry his way into my pants with a report card."

Blushing, he signaled the counterman for a warm-up and read. Ellen plucked out a Lucky, tapped it on the pack, and lit it, sat back to smoke and hum along with Peggy Lee.

He finished and slid the story her way. "Cute."

"Thanks for not being kind." She scooped it up and stuck it back in her handbag. Her nostrils were pinched.

"I don't know what else to say about a lost-dog story, unless the dog winds up getting run over. Oh, on page six you used 'further' when you meant 'farther.' I'm surprised our intrepid instructor missed that; but like you said—"

"You're a bit of a shit, aren't you?"

"You asked for honesty."

"I did not."

He sat back and finished his coffee. "What a relief! I keep hearing the girls back home aren't the same girls I left behind. Good to hear they still don't make sense."

"Just how many girls did you leave behind?"

He put down his cup and counted on his fingers. "Princess Lotus, Vesta von Vix, The Moroccan Man-Eater—"

"Tharp's right. You can't write women."

A female voice interrupted "White Christmas" to announce the store was closing in fifteen minutes. The buzzing on the main floor increased. The counterman rang open the cash register and began counting bills.

"What will you do now?" Ellen asked.

"I'm doing it: writing about purse-snatchings and weddings. Hoping someday they'll coincide. A man needs ambition of some kind."

"I think you should take your agent's advice and write novels."

"*Paperback* novels." He already regretted having told her his professional history. "The difference between them and *Muff Pistols* wouldn't buy you a seat on a streetcar."

"Life's what you make it, my father always said."

"What's he do, run General Motors?"

"He *was* a stevedore, until he blew out an artery at forty, unloading crates of machine parts from Cleveland. He had me primed to be the first female governor of New York. He didn't live to see me cutting tin at Lockheed."

"Don't knock defense work. I keep picturing some schnook of a Jap mechanic trying to turn two wrecked Zeroes into one in flying condition, ducking for cover every time a fresh wave of tin flew over from the West." He glanced at the counterman, who was showing inordinate interest in the watch on his wrist. "What about your mother?"

"Slinging hash at Sing Sing; no fooling. The lifers call her Ma. Makes apple pie from scratch, no cans."

"You interest me. How's she feel about her tin-cutting, secretarial-bound daughter?"

"'As long as you're happy, dear.' I think she wants a son-in-law who's a cross between Albert Schweitzer and J. P. Morgan. What about your parents?"

"My father died in France."

"Fighting?"

"Food poisoning. He went there in 1919 to paint and got hold of the only bowl of bad *vichyssoise* in Paris."

"Luck seems to run in your family. Mother?"

"My aunt who raised me said the influenza took her. I took her word for it; I was two. I prefer to think Mom ran away with the circus, but I'm a hopeless romantic."

"Just a couple of orphans."

He wasn't really listening. "So you think I should go crawling back. 'The Typewriter' isn't *Saturday Evening Post* material?"

"Try the *Post*, sure. *The New Yorker*."

"And after that I'll run for president."

"Who said writing is the only profession where you start at the top and work your way down?"

"Whoever it was probably invented paperbacks."

CHAPTER
EIGHT

The Saturday Evening Post returned "The Typewriter" with a form rejection letter two weeks after he submitted it. *The New Yorker* took another week. When he reread the dog-eared manuscript, he no longer liked it. He circled those passages he might use later and threw away the rest.

He never used any of it, however, and in no time at all the story was forgotten. There was no place for it in his second novel.

It happened this way:

The Woolworth's near P.S. 187 became his rendezvous place with Ellen Curry. It wasn't on his way home from the paper, but she hadn't offered her phone number and he was too rusty at the game to work up the courage to ask. By the time she gave it, the meetings had become a habit. On Tuesdays and Thursdays he left the office just before class let out. She would show him her latest assignment and he would make suggestions that would never occur to Tharp.

A week before Christmas, they waited twenty minutes for a booth. Standing in line, he read a descriptive piece she'd written.

"You need to cut down on the adjectives."

"How can I write description without adjectives?"

"I didn't say don't use any. Three per noun is less effective than one."

"I never thought of it that way."

"Anyway, that's what my editors said. I'm sure it's just a coincidence they paid by the word."

"I should be paying *you*."

"Save your money. You're not really a writer, you know."

"I told you that the first night."

"I saw it the first night. I was afraid if I agreed with you, you'd slap my face."

"Women are always doing that in your stories. I've never slapped anyone. I don't know a woman who has."

"Me neither, come to think. I wrote a lot of scenes I wouldn't now."

A man got up from a booth to pay his check. They took possession and waited while the counterman wiped down the table. When he left, Jacob had an epiphany. "How the hell did you get hold of my stories?"

"My roommate's father died recently. When she went home to help her mother clean out his things, she found boxes of magazines in the garage. He was saving them for the paper drive, but then the war ended. Ann was going to throw them away, but I asked if I could have them. I had a hunch. My favorite is 'Dead Before Dawn.'"

He smiled. "Mine, too. It's the only time an editor used my title."

"Is that the only reason?"

"After I've had a chance to cool off, nothing I write satisfies me. By then it's too late, because the story's already in print and the check's cashed." He paused. "I threw away the typewriter story."

"Oh, you shouldn't have done that!"

"I should never have sent it out. At least this time I spared myself public embarrassment."

"What you're saying is I'm a lousy critic."

"You didn't read the story I had in mind when I wrote it. Nothing ever turns out the way I want."

"You're too hard on yourself."

"Tell that to the *Post* and the *New Yorker*."

"They're not the only magazines in the world."

"They will be, if things go on the way they have. Want to see a movie sometime?"

She paused in the midst of lighting a cigarette, shook out the match. "Did you just ask me for a date? You said it so fast I'm not sure."

"It's like ripping off a Band-Aid; one shrill scream and you're in the clear."

"I'd love to. Feel free to scream any time."

Someone cleared his throat: A man waiting in line with a woman at his side. Jacob and Ellen had finished eating.

As he helped her on with her coat, a familiar-looking color scheme caught his eye. He turned for a better look.

"Son of a bitch."

She turned her head to stare. "What? My arm's tangled in the sleeve."

"Not you." He went to the wooden rack that had replaced the pulp magazines at the end of the counter and snatched out one of the gaudy books on display. It was the Blue Devil Books edition of *Chinese Checkers,* "by Jack Holly."

"Hey, hey!" Ira Winderspear rose into the awkward crouch diners at 21 assumed to greet visitors to their booth. He had a bloody steak in front of him and a napkin tucked under his chin.

Jacob didn't shake his hand. "Talk fast, Ira. Give me one good reason why I shouldn't call the Bunco Squad."

"Hell, kid. I'll give you a thousand." The agent dropped back onto his seat, reached inside a breast pocket, and handed him a check made out to Jacob Heppleman in the amount of $1,089.84. It was signed by Winderspear.

"Your first royalty, kid. I took out my ten percent."

He stared at the check in his hands. "How can there be royalties already? I never got any the first time around."

"Different world, kid. It's almost 1947. Book's in its third printing."

"I never authorized a first."

"That's the thing. I didn't get around to asking Elk not to

publish. Where would I start? 'Heppleman didn't exactly sign the contract'? Un-fucking-professional."

Jacob felt all kinds of a fool, seething in a public place with money in his fist. Still . . . but Winderspear was first to fill the gap in the conversation.

"Listen, kid, I got a meeting uptown like I said on the phone, so we'll save time and say you said you're sorry and I said buy me a beer sometime." He produced a pencil and notebook, scribbled something on a sheet, and tore it off. "He's expecting you at two. Here's the address."

"He who?"

"Jeez, you sound like a cross between a jackass and a hoot owl. Robin Elk, that's who. He's Blue Devil Books."

"You made an appointment without asking me?"

"He wants the meeting. I've been stalling him a couple weeks. Your old number's disconnected. You forgot to give me your new one."

"Why would I fire you and then give you my phone number?"

"How should I know? I told you I'm not used to getting canned. Your luck went south right after, didn't it? Fess up."

He had the evidence of Ellen to refute that; but he wasn't about to share that information. Winderspear misread his silence. "Don't say I didn't warn you."

"What have I got to talk about with Elk? It's your job to dicker with publishers, not mine."

"That's pre-war thinking. These days the writer's part of the package. Look at this guy Stratton, writes the Lash Logan private eye books? Got his ugly kisser on a million back covers. That could be you."

"Who says I want that?"

"So tell Elk. Get going or you'll be late. You don't want to make a bad impression first shot out of the box."

CHAPTER
NINE

He frowned out the cab window. "Are you sure this is the address?"

"It's the one you gave me, Mac. Do I look like the *Manhattan Directory*?"

He paid the driver and got out in front of a rambling Queen Anne house in a neighborhood of them. It was the only one without a FOR RENT sign in any of its windows. There was no commercial sign to identify it as a business.

A typewritten three-by-five card perched above an old-fashioned bell-pull told him to RING THEN ENTER. The bell made a rusty jangle when he tugged on it.

Inside was a foyer, with squares of black and white marble laid corner to corner at his feet and mahogany fretwork carved into swirls suggestive of cinnamon rolls. A young man in horn-rimmed glasses looked up at him from behind a desk lit by a banker's lamp with a green glass shade. He wore a sacksuit and a white shirt buttoned to the neck, no tie. At his elbow was a telephone console with a row of square buttons like accordion keys.

Jacob introduced himself. The young man lifted the handset and tapped a key. He spoke with a slight New England drawl. "Jacob Heppleman for Mr. Elk. Yes." He hung up. "He's expecting you; top of the stairs, first door to the right."

The staircase curved gracefully between polished banisters, with an Oriental runner so thick the treads made no noise under his feet. The door stood open. At a desk sat a woman who might have been related to the young man. She wore a serge business suit, pulled her light brown hair back into a bun, and smiled at him tentatively behind glasses with clear frames. "Go right on in, Mr. Holly."

"Heppleman."

"Of course." She turned to a battleship gray Smith-Corona on a drawleaf and began typing at Sten gun pace.

A glazed cabinet stood next to the door behind her desk. The covers of uncirculated paperbacks leered out through the glass, beetle-browed men watching frowzy women taking off their clothes in one seedy hotel room after another, usually with a fully erect handgun present. *Chinese Checkers* occupied the central position.

Subtle.

The door was paneled, with a brass plate engraved PRIVATE. He twisted the knob and opened it.

He'd fully expected something crude behind the elegant front, a creature sprung from the same gene pool as the Cro-Magnons in the glass case, with a cigarette pasted to his lip and soup stains on his tie.

"This is indeed a pleasure, Mr. Holly. I've been looking forward to it ever so long."

The man who stood to greet him was so unexpected he forgot to correct the use of names. Robin Elk was his age—possibly a year younger—and spoke with an upper-class British accent. He wore his blond hair in a pompadour, but shaven close at the temples, and Harris tweeds over an argyle sweater and a bow tie. He came out from behind his desk and they shook hands. The publisher's grip was strong, but not competitive. He gripped a cherrywood cane with a silver handle. Jacob noticed he wore paper slippers and shuffled slightly when he walked. "You served in the American armed forces, I understand."

"The army. Yourself?"

"RAF. Shot down over Cherbourg in '43, spent the next two years in a Stalag. Flatirons." He tapped one foot gingerly with the cane's rubber tip. "You'd think the buggers would've updated their methods after the first go."

"Whatever brought you to the States?"

"Your postwar prosperity. It's an American invention. Back home they're still queuing up before dawn for a bit of ham. No future there for a fellow with ambition and bad memories. Can I interest you in a bracer?" He shuffled back to the desk and flipped the switch on an intercom. "Alice, what's in the larder?"

"A bit early for me, thanks. Coffee, if you have it."

"Right-o. Cream and sugar?"

"A little of both."

"Coffee, the works," Elk told Alice.

"Two cups?" The voice belonged to the woman in the outer office.

"Please." He switched off, winked at his guest. "If it weren't for the damned tea, we'd still have an empire." He waved him toward a sitting area that resembled the reading room in a gentlemen's club. Leather armchairs shared a walnut smoking stand next to shelves of gold-stamped volumes on the wall.

They sat. Nothing about the room indicated it belonged to a publisher of two-bit paperbacks. A framed panoramic photograph of young men in fleece-lined jackets standing and kneeling in front of a British Spitfire at some aerodrome hung above a stone fireplace with logs crackling on the grate. Elk charged a blackened brier pipe with coarse tobacco and set it burning with a bundle of matches. A sweetish, tarry scent permeated the room. "What's your pleasure? A bowl? My own blend. Cigars? Cigarettes? My God, I sound like the girl in a nightclub."

"Thanks. I don't smoke."

Blond brows rose. "You're the first Yank I've met who came back without the craving. What did you do with the cartons that came with your K rations?"

"Traded them to smokers for extra rations."

"And Napoleon called *us* a nation of shopkeepers. Well, we shan't compare war stories. Tell me a bit about yourself. In turn, you can ask me anything you like."

There wasn't much to tell, he learned as he told it: Raised on a farm, which he hated. Parents deceased. The fight with the foreman that led him to the drugstore periodicals section. His enlistment, discharge, the unwanted war novel.

"I can't say I'm surprised," Elk said to that. "I'm sick of the subject myself. How are you paying the bills?"

"Newspaper work."

"Where would I find your byline?"

"Nowhere." He explained his job on the rewrite desk.

"No new attempts at fiction?"

"One. You wouldn't be interested. No one else was."

"Try me."

He told him about "The Typewriter," leaving out the truth behind the idea.

"Hm."

Alice came in carrying a tray with a silver carafe, a matching creamer, sugar cubes in a china bowl, and two cups and saucers with the same pattern, a coat-of-arms of some kind, all of which she set on a low table with claw feet. Her skirt was knee-length, a new development in fashion. Muscular calves. "I'll be mother," said Elk, when she raised the carafe. She put it down and took herself out, not before gifting Jacob with a reassuring smile.

He took advantage of the break while Elk poured to ask a question that had been vexing him. "Why a blue devil?"

The publisher chuckled and sat back cradling his cup and saucer. "We started with red—the shock effect, you know. Edgy. Can't impress a postwar readership with the same staid tactics that worked in the past. The first design looked like something out of Bosch; fire shooting from the nostrils, that sort of rot. But it smacked of the Plague and the Inquisition, and after six years of conflict and pestilence it wasn't the way to go. Also there was the Catholic Church to consider.

"So we changed his color and extinguished the flames. Baby blankets are blue; so are skies and the little boy under the haystack. Also we made the horns smaller. Looks like Bambi, don't you think? Yes."

"What happened to edgy?"

"You've seen our covers. Why beat a dead horse?"

Jacob sank two cubes in his coffee and colored it with cream. "There's no torture scene in *Chinese Checkers*."

"But there was! You've forgotten the story the old Mandarin in the junk shop told, about coming to this country to flee the Tongs."

"He's a minor character. He has one scene."

"And an excellent scene it was. I quite liked the book. So do the readers. You got your royalty check?"

"I thought at first it was a mistake. How many copies do you have to sell at two bits a pop to pay the author a thousand dollars?"

"Twenty thousand. The first printing was ten. That's why we went back to press. Six months from now you'll receive another check, and if it isn't bigger than the first, I'll go back home and work for the admiral."

"The admiral?"

"My father. He was dead set on my joining the Royal Navy. But sons are placed on this earth to disappoint their fathers. He owns a publishing firm in Knightsbridge, cranking out matched sets of Dickens and Thackeray bound in half-calf; the sort of rot freshly knighted war profiteers buy by the yard to appear literate. The plan for me was to return from the jolly old high seas with the rank of commander, apprentice to the editor-in-chief for a year or two, then put the old boy out to pasture—with a pension, of course—and move into the big office overlooking the V-and-A. Instead I sank my trust fund into a third-class steamship ticket and this barn, with a bit left over for staffing and a printing plant on Long Island."

"Weren't you afraid that would kill the admiral?"

"Oh, he's tough old Edwardian stock. It would take more than the Blitz to make a dent in those iron sides. Although I daresay if he knew I'd booked third-class he might lock himself in the wine cellar and never come out."

Jacob smiled, thawing somewhat. He was beginning to like this man. He didn't quite buy the port-and-polo image Elk seemed to be working overtime to sell; it was all too spot-on, like something from Evelyn Waugh. But there was a naïveté about him that put a skeptic off-guard. As well be suspicious of a child who would do anything to please.

Then again, clever confidence men seldom *acted* shifty.

Jacob returned his cup and saucer to the tray, then sat back, legs crossed. "I'm trying to wrap my mind around this sudden success. I was told veterans and their wives are too busy starting families to read for pleasure."

"A judgment made in haste. There's always confusion when the swords are being beaten back into plowshares, or however the saying goes: A period of adjustment. When I was a prisoner of war I became quite chummy with a lieutenant with your Army Air Corps." He pronounced it *leftenant*. "Red Cross relief packages were few and far between—the German black market thrived on them—but I took an interest in the Armed Forces editions he received: You know the ones?"

"They were one of the things I traded cigarettes for."

"Quite. I read them, mysteries and cowboy stories and such. Needless to say few would pass muster at Elk & Ridpath, but they helped us through a great ordeal, boredom being first and foremost. The lieutenant and I exchanged addresses. In our letters after the war we discussed those cheap paperbound books, which he said had begun to appear in American apothecaries, of all places."

"Drugstores, yes."

"Hm. He said Yanks were buying them straight off the racks, a half-dozen at a time, tucking them under their arms like sausages during a run on the butcher's. They sold for a quarter, the longer ones fifty pence, so the customer could be reasonably sure there'd be no unpleasant surprise when he unloaded his plunder at the counter.

"That was the extent of my market research, but it's a damn

sight more thorough than anything my father attempted. D'you know, publishing is the only industry in the U.K. whose executives have no bloody idea who buys their product? Shameful. But try persuading those hidebound traders to re-examine their traditional methods. So I copped a Pilgrim."

"I'm sorry?"

"Bolted, dear boy, like those stalwarts who set sail aboard the *Mayflower* bound for liberty and free enterprise. American investors are always looking for the next new thing; and they're suckers for a West End accent. You aren't offended, I hope?"

"I might be, if I were an investor."

"I'd have done the thing on my own, but distribution is a complicated business over here. What at first looks like a bargain can put you in debt to the sort of villain who always gets his comeuppance in the final chapters of the very books we're publishing."

"In other words you want to steer clear of the people who own the jukebox and vending-machine routes." Jacob bent his nose to one side with a finger.

"Succinctly put. There you have it." Elk spread his white palms. "The reading public is insatiable. Our industry has pillaged literature as far back as Homer—remind me to send you our edition of *The Iliad,* abridged, of course; our Helen bears a strong resemblance to Betty Grable—and is desperate for more product. Blue Devil will be the first publisher to issue paperback originals, never before seen in print. A pioneer. And I want you aboard the flagship."

CHAPTER
TEN

Jacob laughed. He couldn't help himself. "Are you sure you didn't serve in the Royal Navy?"

Elk touched his bow tie. The writer would come to recognize this gesture as a sign of discomfort, and anticipate an immediate change of tone, if not subject.

"Needless to say, we require writers who are willing to join us in our enterprise. The established ones are complacent, and what they write is far too sedate for this market. Come in." Someone had knocked.

A middle-aged man in his shirtsleeves entered carrying a large portfolio bound in tattered black cloth. A cigarette wobbled on his lower lip and sparks from it—or its predecessors—had burned tiny holes in his checked shirt. His body was a perfect tube, the shoulders as narrow as the waist, and the cheekstrap bones of the skull under his skin stood out like umbrella staves.

His appearance was the first indication the rambling Victorian mansion contained more than just Elk, Alice, and the young man in the foyer.

"You wanted to see this the minute it came in." The man untied the string on the portfolio and opened it, holding it in front of him like a sandwich board.

"Jack Holly, Skip Glaser. Skip's our art director."

Jacob nodded, Glaser having no free hand to shake. He couldn't picture a man who looked less like a Skip.

"Welcome aboard." The art director's attention remained on Elk's face.

Clipped to the edges of the portfolio was a flat-finish photographic print, apparently full size, of an oil painting, obviously intended for a paperback cover. Refreshingly, this one contained no women, in undress or otherwise. The man in the center was seen in full length, upside-down. His arms were splayed, one knee bent, and his mouth twisted into a rictus of terror. Behind him—beneath him, really—yawned rows of windows stacked one atop another, plummeting toward the sidewalk far below. He hung suspended, a dozen stories from death.

What struck Jacob was the sole of the man's right shoe directly in the foreground, huge, disproportionate to the rest of his body: It seemed to stick out of the illustration in third-dimension, pleading for Jacob to seize it and haul him to safety.

"Splendid. Perhaps a bit more in the expression. He looks annoyed, as if he's just dropped his pencil instead of twelve floors. What do you think, Jack?"

"Please call me Jacob."

"As you wish; in private, of course. I'm genuinely interested in your opinion as an artist yourself."

He tabled the business of the *nom de plume* for later. "He looks frightened enough. His predicament's clear. Why telegraph it and insult the customer?"

"Just a bit more, I think. Thank you, Skip."

The art director closed the portfolio and left.

Elk brushed imaginary ash from his sweater. "I understand your point of view, Jack—Jacob, pardon me. This isn't the time for restraint. I want to make the person who sees that cover reach out automatically to catch him, the way early French cinema audiences leapt backwards when a train seemed to be thundering out of the screen into their laps."

Once again Jacob adjusted his opinion of the publisher. He himself had wanted to do just that, save the poor wretch. It made the audience part of the drama.

Elk said, "We're calling the book *Smash Hit.* Do you know Hank Stratton?"

"Not personally. I thought he was with Bannerman."

"He was, until we told him we were starting with a print run of one hundred thousand. It will be the first paperback original featuring Lash Logan. We're quite excited about it."

"What's it about?"

"Haven't the foggiest. He hasn't written it yet."

"Then, how did you know—?"

"The illustration? That was Skip's brainstorm. I'm confident Stratton will follow it up. It was good enough for Dickens. *The Pickwick Papers* started out as a collection of random watercolors by an artist who committed suicide. The story came later."

He wanted to ask if the man killed himself before he read the book or after; but he was thinking of Stratton, not Dickens.

"I thought private eyes were dying with the pulps."

"The pulps at their boldest never let the detective grapple with a naked woman, or strangle a pander to death with his bare hands."

"Another pioneer." This time he couldn't hold back.

But the publisher seemed unperturbed. "When this one comes out, schoolboys across America will be reading it under the blankets with a flashlight. Eveready should pay us a dividend based on all those extra battery sales."

"When I write about a brute and a sadist, he won't be the hero."

"It would never occur to me to ask you to violate your principles. Personally, I think Stratton's cretinous, and his character's a thumping fascist; but we need the sales. The market's overcrowded with snoops in trench coats. The only reason he's so popular is because he's . . ." He trailed off, his grasp of American vernacular having failed him.

"Gimmicky."

Elk beamed. "Precisely! A blatant imitation would fool no one. Even if it worked, the result would be a disaster, dividing the readership and harming sales. We must agree upon another path. That typewriter story you mentioned gave me an idea. Why not a series about an honorable thief?"

"I think Robin Hood beat you to it."

"How rapidly you thought of him. He's my namesake. Perhaps the fabulists who improved upon the scrofulous original expressed these same doubts. It wasn't a new idea even at the time.

"But, no, that business of robbing the rich to give to the poor flies too close to Marxism for comfort. The HUAC isn't a tiger we want to poke. *Your* character—what's his name, by the way?"

"Herbert Jackdaw." He remembered coming up with it on impulse, reversing his own initials.

Elk appeared to consider, then shook his head. "Some kind of raucous bird, named after President Hoover. That's two strikes against it. We'll find something better. Your character seeks redemption and reform. Why not take it a step further and have him go after his own former underworld brethren? Clandestinely, of course; the law must never know it has an ally in him. The fact that he's wanted himself would add to the suspense. At all times he must look ahead and behind."

"That's the premise of *The Creeper.*"

"Radio-show hokum. We won't bother about cloaks and masks and that rubbish; the comic books have already appropriated it. You must have a death wish in order to compete with them."

"Didn't you just say you wanted boys for your audience?"

"I said that's who Stratton appeals to. Workingmen are the target, truck drivers and factory drones, those fellows you worked with under that contemptible foreman, who come home dragging their lunch pails and want nothing but a beer, a comfortable chair, and something to read that won't challenge their intellects while they're waiting for supper. Men you understand, having been one yourself."

He wasn't sure how to take that. Either Elk had no idea of the effect he had on people or he was smirking at him from behind a mask of innocence.

"What I want," the publisher went on, "is a professional criminal in ordinary street dress, employing the same tactics to support the law he once used to circumvent it."

The idea had appeal, but he wasn't ready to cede the point. "That's what *you* want. How do you know it's what these workingmen you're talking about want?"

"*They* don't know, yet. It's our job to tell them. You must trust me on that. It's a publishing maxim, as old as movable type."

"Can I think about it?"

"Please. While you do, I'd admire to read the story. Will you send it to me?"

"I threw it away. I'm not sure I kept the carbon."

"Can you look?"

"The protagonist is nothing like the man you described. The story has problems of its own apart from that."

"I'll remember you said that, and withhold criticism."

He was on the point of declaring he was sure he'd destroyed the carbon, but the beseeching expression on the Englishman's frank features gave him pause. "I'll see what I can do. One thing. How far along is that second printing of *Chinese Checkers*?"

"It's in the chase now. Why?"

"I want to sponge out all that garbage about inherently wicked Asians. I fought side-by-side with some of them, and I can tell you they come in all packages, just like the rest of us."

Elk kneaded the head of his stick. "That sounds extensive. We'll have to charge you for any changes that come to more than ten percent the cost of production."

"I'm aware of that."

"Fabulous. Let me see you out."

As Jacob entered the outer office, Elk holding the door and leaning on his cane, Alice stopped chugging away at her typewriter to turn their way and smile, pushing her glasses up her nose. In the instant her eyes weren't distorted by the thick lenses, all physical similarity to the young man in the foyer vanished. It struck Jacob she bore a closer resemblance to the blondes on most of the Blue Devil covers. He wondered if Elk was economizing by asking his secretary to double as a model. And he wondered how the body under the mannish suit compared to those of the near-naked women in all those shabby bedrooms. The impure thought made his cheeks burn.

"Here. No one leaves empty-handed." Tucking the cane under one arm, Elk opened the glazed cabinet and began scooping books from inside. He shoved a stack of seven or eight into Jacob's hands. "For your entertainment, but also for study. See what the others are doing."

"I was under the impression you liked the way I write. If you expect me to change—"

"Good Lord, no! Montgomery didn't stop being Montgomery when he studied Rommel's strategy. And he certainly didn't win El Alamein by using the same methods that worked in the Argonne wood. I want the author of *Chinese Checkers*. *Blue Devil* wants the postwar model."

Jacob gained some insight in that moment. Whenever Robin Elk spoke of Blue Devil Books as if it were separate from himself, something vaguely unpleasant was in store.

CHAPTER ELEVEN

They saw *It's a Wonderful Life* at The Rialto, a neighborhood theater not far from her apartment. Ellen thought James Stewart was good-looking, which answered Jacob's questions about what she saw in him ("gangling" was the adjective he heard often). He walked her home afterward. The lights of the marquee went out and foot traffic fell off as they left the block. They passed dimly lit store windows with Christmas displays behind them.

A light snow fell, but it was a mild evening for December and the flakes dissolved when they touched down. He was comfortable in his wool-felt hat and light topcoat, she fetching in a knitted beret and red suede jacket with a monkey collar. He held her gloved hand in his bare one.

"I was actually disappointed at the end," he said. "Pottersville looked like a fun place on a Saturday night."

"It was Gomorrah. I'll take Bedford Falls."

"Great place—for ninety minutes. I went to school in a town just like it. Couldn't wait to get out, just like George Bailey. Worse happened there than in Pottersville."

"There is no Pottersville."

"Sure there is."

"I think you missed the point of the movie."

"Tarzan's chimp couldn't have missed the point of that movie." They walked a block in silence. "Tharp asked me out again."

"Don't let him take you to *It's a Wonderful Life*. He'll just say Frank Capra stole it from Dickens."

"You know I turned him down."

He squeezed her hand. "What's your roommate up to?"

"In bed, spraying germs like Flit. She's got a cold."

"Rats. I was going to ask if you had eggnog."

"Just some old buttermilk. A shot of bourbon might kill the taste, but what will we do with Ann?"

"If we were characters in a book and Robin Elk were publishing, we'd be plotting her murder right now."

Her building was a brownstone with a globe glowing above the front door. She slipped off a glove to use her key. He took the hand, put it behind his neck, and kissed her. When he finished, she nestled her head under his chin. "When are you going to show me where you live?"

"When I'm living someplace better."

"As bad as that?"

"It belongs on the cover of a Blue Devil book."

He'd taken an apartment eight blocks from *The Greenwich Clock*. It was smaller than the one he'd moved out of, so he'd set up the Remington Streamliner on the kitchen table on a straw mat, which he could shove aside when he ate, and used the oven for a file cabinet. The racks kept folders vertical. He'd found the carbon of "The Typewriter" in one, put it in a stamped envelope, and sent it to the Queen Anne house from the box on the corner.

Whoever had used the stove before him had lived on a steady diet of cauliflower and cabbage. The stench was ineradicable. In winter with the windows shut, it mixed with the scorched-metal smell from the radiator; an evil blend. But rents in the Village were reasonable, and walking to and from work saved bus fare. The money from *Chinese Checkers* was in the bank, earmarked for expenses. There was no telling how long his job would last, and despite Elk's assurances, he didn't expect another check in six months or ever.

The place was comfortable enough. The cockroaches weren't overbold, and the El was far enough away the glasses stayed put on the shelves when the train rumbled past. But it was no place to entertain a young woman.

He wasn't sure he wanted to. Four years spent no more than a yard apart from another human being (particularly the G.I. variety that snored and farted in its sleep and griped incessantly when awake) made a man jealous of his privacy. He laughed at corny jokes on the radio, played the same dumb tunes he'd enjoyed before the war on a secondhand phonograph, and when he woke up at midnight realizing he'd forgotten supper, threw a gristly ham steak into a pan and stank up the joint further, without apology. Modern comforts aside, it was a caveman's life, and none of the fossils left behind showed signs of depression or suicide.

He knew it wouldn't last, this satisfaction with existence on his own terms, but he meant to get everything out of it before it staled. He'd never be able to explain it to Ellen in terms she'd understand; to women, "alone" meant "lonely," and anyone who said he enjoyed solitude was either a liar or a selfish jerk. That was one bridge he wouldn't burn. He'd want company eventually.

But how long would her patience hold out?

Christmas Day passed quietly. Ellen spent it in Ossining with her mother, who had leave from the prison cafeteria; he'd thought that was a rib, like his fantasy about *his* mother joining the circus, but it turned out "Ma" Curry had been there longer than many of the lifers. His relationship with Ellen hadn't reached the point where meeting the parents was an obstacle that couldn't be avoided—a fact that relieved them both, although neither would admit it aloud. They'd already exchanged safe gifts—a necktie for him, a set of lace handkerchiefs for her. Late in the morning she called to tell him merry Christmas and express concern that he might celebrate it with macaroni and cheese and a beer instead of turkey with all the trimmings, but he said he was treating himself to steak and potatoes and a glass of Dago Red.

"Festive."

"Anything fancier would louse up my filing system."

"You haven't had Ma's Christmas dinner. She can't fix it to serve less than eighty, so make room in the icebox for leftovers."

After they hung up, he opened a can of sardines and ate while reading one of the books Elk had given him, washing down the oily fish with milk straight from the bottle. He'd been so busy at the paper, writing about shoplifters and fires caused by Christmas candles, he hadn't had a chance to stop at the market.

He turned off the radio while Jack Benny was haggling with St. Nick over a strand of imitation pearls for Mary Livingstone. The dialogue was a distraction.

He'd begun to form grudging admiration for the writing that made its way between Blue Devil's garish covers. Some was dross: *Baby, It's Murder* was warmed-over Chandler, and *The Berserkers of Thrym* was a bald steal from Lovecraft. But in Don Ogilvie's *Bump in the Night* and J. B. Collier's *Guns at Diablo* he found disciplined prose and snap characterizations that captured in a phrase what Tolstoy and Flaubert had spent paragraphs accomplishing, at a pace Jacob associated with the short story.

He'd found, when necessity such as a research trip to the main branch of the New York Public Library meant a bus ride, that Lyle Hobart's 170-page *Killers' Code* fit neatly into an inside breast pocket, and that reading it shortened a journey of many blocks to moments. When his stop came up, it was an annoying interruption.

The day after Christmas was a Thursday. The phone rang as he struggled into his galoshes for the trek to work. A steady snow was falling.

"Jacob? Elk. Is it a bad time?"

He wondered for a moment where the publisher had gotten his number. Then he remembered he'd included it with his address on "The Typewriter." "It is, I'm afraid. I'm late for work."

"I'll be brief. Your story was all right, so far as it went. I think you should keep one character and forget about the rest."

"Changing his name from Herbert Jackdaw, of course."

"Actually, I didn't care for him. Too passive. We got bushels of returns on *Hamlet* because he didn't kill Claudius in Act Two. Your pawnbroker's the bloke we want."

"He only had three lines."

"Leaving a stronger impression than your vacillating writer. He mustn't be legitimate, however. A dealer in dubious merchandise—got religion, of course, and now uses his shop to trap thieves and killers. Think of the arsenal he has on hand, firearms and apple-corers and such! What's the colorful underworld term for a man in that trade?"

"Fence."

"That's it! *The Fence.* Marvelous title. Tell me you can write it in six months and I'll begin the dreary negotiations with Wind-erspear."

"That's tight. I don't even know how a fence works."

"Surely a longtime New Yorker knows someone who knows someone. Back home we were under the impression you all had bookies on retainer."

His gaze fell on the sleek Remington crouched on the table. "I may know someone, but I doubt he'll cooperate."

"Rubbish! Who doesn't want to be the hero in a book?"

———

A doctor's black leather satchel occupied the portable typewrit-er's old spot in the pawnshop window, its top spread open to display the instruments and bottles inside. With a writer's cu-riosity, Jacob pondered the circumstances that would compel a physician to hock the tools of his profession. The obvious con-clusion, that it was stolen, he rejected as lacking tragedy and therefore useless.

It was Saturday. He'd half hoped the shop would be closed for the Sabbath; but either the owner was a Gentile or not Ortho-dox. He took a deep breath and pushed the bell.

The buzzer sounded angrier than before, the clunk of the lock releasing itself more like a cell door slamming shut. He tugged on the handle and slid inside quickly.

"Yes-s?"

Merchandise had come and gone, but nothing about the man behind the counter had changed, not the Edwardian sleeve-protectors nor the eyeshade that made his pinched face bilious nor the crooked bow tie that looked like the stalled propeller of a Navy Corsair. Then recognition swam to the surface of the mud-colored eyes.

"You!" He reached under the counter.

"Unarmed!" Jacob threw up his hands, a crisp fifty-dollar bill clutched in one.

The revolver came up. "You think a thief can buy his way out of jail? That window alone cost me ten bucks!"

"I'll make good on all of it. I never planned to rob you. That crack about veterans made me mad. The pistol wasn't loaded. I was drunk when I threw that brick. My name is Jacob Heppleman. I'm a writer."

The proprietor held on to the revolver, groped for the candlestick phone on the counter with his other hand. "You'll get plenty of time to write; ten to fifteen years."

"I want to show you something. It's in my pocket."

"I seen it already. I got one, too, don't forget." He rattled the prong. "Operator! Get me the police."

"Not the gun. A book. *My* book. *Chinese Checkers.* I'm getting paid to write another. It's about a pawnbroker, like yourself."

"So what, you going to write my life story?"

The phone was ringing on the other end, a sinister purring. He spoke quickly.

"Subjects don't get paid. Collaborators do. We'll split the profits. This is on account." He laid the fifty on the counter.

The pawnbroker chewed on a cheek, caving in his narrow face on that side. "How do I know you're a writer?"

"Who else would steal a typewriter?"

He hung up just as a voice came on the line. He pocketed the bill, took *Chinese Checkers*, riffled the pages, slapped it down. "I got no time for yarns. Made-up people doing made-up things. What's the point?"

"Search me. But if we make a deal, you'll have a hundred extra bucks in your pocket."

"That don't sound like no split."

The proprietor's name was Linus Pickering. The conference took a half hour, interrupted from time to time by customers pawning gifts or personal property to pay Christmas bills. Jacob made a final offer: eighty–twenty of the advance in his favor.

Pickering looked as if he'd gnaw a hole in his cheek. Then he ducked through a beaded curtain in back, to return a minute later carrying something. He lifted it onto the counter with little apparent effort. "You forgot this."

Jacob looked at the pebbled-black case that belonged to the Remington. Then he shook hands with the pawnbroker.

PART TWO

1946–1947
TWO BITS A POP

CHAPTER
TWELVE

"I'm not a Jew," Pickering said. "It's an advantage, let me tell you. Guy has a date set up for Saturday night, he can't wait till Sunday to pawn his watch, so he comes here. The days of taking a dame bicycling in Central Park went down with the *Arizona*."

Jacob tried not to sound impatient. "I saw *The Lost Weekend* in the service. Ray Milland hasn't a cent to pay for a drink, so he walks all over town looking for a shop that's open on the Sabbath." He wanted to know about fence work, but so far the conversation was all small talk.

"I saw that one." The dull eyes brightened. "Hey, he was trying to hock his typewriter! I guess you and me were meant to partner up."

"A match made in Hollywood." He waited. "Tell me about the hockshop business."

"I never use that word. It sounds common. You see those three balls hanging outside? Every honest pawnbroker in town has 'em. They go back to the Medicis in Italy, a family of physicians originally. The balls represent pills. It's a respectable profession, older than the presidency, and a damn sight less crooked."

"I didn't mean to offend."

"Undertakers."

"What?"

Pickering repeated it. "There's crooks for you. They had their way, you could fit every pawnshop in the city in one block down by the garment district. They got first dibs on the estates: Victrolas, fainting-couches, Persian rugs, pump organs, oil lamps wired electric. That's why their visitors' rooms always look like Queen Victoria's shithouse and smell like old people. The rest they sell on the side. Think about it. There's always a used-furniture store next to a funeral home. Buzzards.

"We're a close-knit group as a rule," he went on: "If a guy can't unload something in his neighborhood, there's always one who can't keep it in stock where he is, so he gets it wholesale. Everyone benefits, no one feels cheated. But I don't do business with undertakers. They're always pawning rings and watches, stuff they took off stiffs before they nailed the lid shut. Sometimes they don't even bother to scrape off the pancake makeup. Ever shake a funeral director's hand? Clean as a whistle and pink as a monkey's butt. It's the formaldehyde." He shuddered.

They were sitting in the little room on the other side of the beaded curtain, Pickering in a brown mohair armchair worn shiny on the arms, Jacob on a piano stool. He couldn't swivel more than six inches in any direction without bumping into toasters, portable radios, candlesticks, sets of silverware in rosewood boxes, bridal gowns, pocket watches, picture frames, racks of pipes, overcoats, shotguns, and pile upon pile of military decorations. There was an ancient black iron safe that would contain the especially valuable items, gold fixtures and jewelry, with a fringed shawl on top of it and on top of that a brass lamp in the shape of a wicked-looking cherub. A six-foot birchwood canoe swung on ropes from the ceiling. Mildew and dry-rot hung heavy in the air.

None of it was junk. The appliances would all be in working order, the silver sterling, the firearms clean and oiled, the canoe seaworthy. At a glance, including what was probably in the safe, Jacob calculated the man was sitting on a fortune in convertible assets. Manhattan millionaires came in all packages. The average thief would walk past Linus Pickering and Ira Winderspear without a glance, and pass up the score of a lifetime.

"I don't deal in hot merchandise," Pickering said. "I never saw the percentage. In the Depression there was always something coming in, you paid a nickel on the dollar and stood pat. Nobody ever redeemed anything, and after six months you marked it all up and stuck it in the window. Sooner or later somebody with dough came around. Wartime was tough, sure. Everybody was hanging on to what he had, fixing up, making do. Some days it didn't pay to open up.

"Couple of guys went over to the black market, sold tires and gasoline out the back door. Dumb. Who wants J. Edgar Hoover on their neck? I sweated it out. Man comes in with a brand-new suitcase, I know right away he boosted it from a luggage shop. Him I don't give the time of day."

Jacob didn't believe him; if corruption had a patron saint, he would look, talk, and dress like Linus Pickering. "Tell me about the ones who went over to the black market."

"No names, understand."

"Understood."

"You meet folks from all over in this business. Every rung on the ladder. Winos, sure, sell Grandma's spoons for the price of a bottle. Spoiled rich kids, too: Dad cut off their allowance for wrecking the Cadillac, they swap gold cuff links, a cashmere sportcoat for chickenfeed or they can't go to the Copa. Junior execs, into the shylocks for a bundle: Season tickets to Yankee Stadium. Some swells, the market took a dive, they can't cover the margin. 'Take good care of the wife's mink coat, willya?' Housewives, they blew the household expenses at the track, here's the old wedding ring. Rackets guys, one week they're wiping their asses with five-spots, next week they can't buy a cuppa Joe. I got enough custom-made silk shirts still in the box to dress a faggots' convention.

"Fella came in once with two hundred grand in diamonds and pearls tied in a handkerchief, swear to Christ. He was squirting sweat, glancing back over his shoulder like a crook in a Porky

Pig cartoon. I told him to get out before I called the cops. He skedaddled. Later I found out he was ten grand in the red to a gambler—a lousy ten g's!—and cleaned out the safe-deposit box where his wife kept her valuables to buy himself into the clear. Had no idea what they were worth, she'd gotten them as gifts from her first husband, a stockbroker. The chump was too embarrassed to ask her for the money.

"Kicker is, not one dame in a hundred would blow the whistle on her husband. She'd've dropped by to redeem her stuff. At two-percent interest, I'd clear four large the first twenty-four hours. But I shooed the guy out."

"Any legitimate pawnbroker would have done the same."

"Think so? Depends on where you're at, I guess. Only then you wouldn't be legit, would you?"

"Those are all good stories, and I can use some, especially the one about the man with the jewels. But I want to hear about the dealers who *aren't* legit."

"I'm coming to that. Wet your whistle?" Pickering got up, rearranged some bric-a-brac, and scooped up a glass demijohn half-full of brown liquid. "It looks like shellac, but they wouldn't be ashamed to serve it at the Waldorf. A tenant in a building I own makes it in her kitchen from dandelions she picks on Staten Island."

"I'll try a taste." The atmosphere in the room was getting close. If the conversation didn't get more interesting, he'd been thinking of ending it and stopping for a drink on the way home.

His host found two cut-crystal glasses and filled them. "Forty dollars a set uptown," he said, striking a chime off one with a fingernail. "Here I can't give 'em away. You should have to show a passport when you cross Fourteenth. Here's to crime." He drank.

Jacob sipped, rested his glass on his thigh—and left it there. It tasted like carbolic fermented in sugar.

Pickering picked up where he'd left off. "With that kind of traffic going on all the time, you hear things. One Hung Lo in Chinatown buys a house in Westchester, Joe Greaseball on Mulberry's driving a brand-new Bentley, Busy Izzie over on First Avenue sets up his old lady in a crib in Miami. I'm making up names here, mixing up addresses. I don't approve, but I'm no rat.

"They went into the war straight as a donkey's dick, then somebody sold 'em a barrel of molasses or a set of spark plugs still in the box, and somebody else offered 'em twice what they paid. No going back after that. The war ends, rationing's over, they miss those quick profits they don't have to pay taxes on because it was all in cash, no receipts. So the first time some jasper shows up looking back over his shoulder and carrying a shitload of tiaras and bracelets tied in a hanky—well, they don't show him the door, and it don't have to be they came from his wife."

"I'd like to visit one of these places."

A lump of dandelion wine got swallowed. "No dice. What'd I just say?"

"Nobody has to know you told me. Nobody has to know *I* know. I'd just like to go in and browse around, see what a fencing operation looks like."

"It looks just like mine. You think the customers all wear striped jerseys and little black masks like on the Get Out of Jail card?"

At the mention of a card, Jacob set his glass on the floor, got up from the piano stool, and fished one out of his wallet. He'd had them printed—after much deliberation and an uneasy night's sleep—with the name Jack Holly. "You can reach me here if you change your mind."

The pawnbroker glanced at it, then stuck it in a pocket of his ash-upholstered vest. "Jesus. I thought you guys just made stuff up."

"That was before the war. I even wrote about *that* once, for *Battlefield,* before I knew what combat was like. I don't think I could even read the story now."

"I don't come through, our deal's off, that it?"

Jacob shook his head. "A deal's a deal. But you want it to sell, right? You don't want to be stuck with a bunch of books like you're stuck with those crystal glasses."

Pickering had raised his for another drink. Now he held it up to eye level and studied the specks floating in the wine. "Okay. Since you put it so I can understand it, I'll think about it."

CHAPTER
THIRTEEN

On New Year's Eve, he rented a tux and asked Ellen to go dancing with him at the Plaza. Her roommate, Ann, answered her door. She was short, plump, and cheerful; either she'd gotten over her father's recent death or she was good at concealing grief. She wore her brown hair short. Ellen had said they'd worked in the same defense plant, and Ann was haunted by stories of women who got their hair caught in machinery, with grim results. She wore a sweater with a cat dressed like Santa Claus on it, a pleated skirt, bobby sox, and saddle shoes.

"Shakespeare. We meet at last." She took his hand and gave it a tomboyish pump. "Don't knock the getup. Frankie's singing at the Apollo. I've got a standing-room ticket. You look like Fred Astaire."

He tugged at his wing collar. "I feel more like Bela Lugosi. Who designed these things?"

"Payback for the brassiere. Come in and get drunk."

It was his first time in the apartment. It was an efficiency place like his, only with a twin bed in addition to a Murphy in the wall. The kitchen appliances were spotless, the laminated table shining, with a red-and-green runner down the center and two mismatched chairs drawn up to it. The living-room area consisted of a sofa, a console radio, an overstuffed chair, and a coffee table holding up a bottle of gin and a six-pack of Coke. On the radio a tinny band played a jump tune in some ballroom downtown.

"She's in the bathroom getting dressed. Gin rickey?" Ann got a clean glass from a cupboard and set it down next to one half-filled with pale red-brown liquid.

"Heavy on the rickey. The night's young." He set a gaily wrapped box on the coffee table.

She splashed Coke on top of a half-inch of gin and added two ice cubes from a bucket. "Clean hands, promise."

He tried not to think of undertakers' hands, *clean as a whistle and pink as a monkey's butt,* and raised the glass. "A lasting peace?"

"The war ended too soon for me. Lost my job to a vet. No offense." She drank off what was in her glass.

He wondered how long Ellen would be.

Ann sat on the sofa, crossing chubby legs. "I dated a writer: He wrote jingles. 'R-O-L-O-F-F; roll off the dirt the Roloff way,'" she sang in a harsh contralto. "Know it?"

"I was probably overseas at the time."

"It sold about a million kitchen mops. I got a free one out of the deal."

"Any good?"

"I used it once, then threw it away and went back to the old-fashioned rag kind. Still, it hung around longer than Henry. The jingle writer?"

He took a sip, purely to sneak a glance at his watch.

"I guess he wasn't the McCoy. Ell says you write books. I thought you'd have gray hair and smoke a pipe."

"Sorry to disappoint."

She squinted. "Don't get testy, Junior. I'm the mother hen in this arrangement. Ell lost the love of her life to the service. It's my job to spare her from disappointment." She poured herself another rickey.

This was news; but he didn't want to hear it from Ann. He sat in the armchair, watching her. If she lost fifteen pounds and bleached her hair, she could pose for a Blue Devil cover, with a gat in her hand instead of a glass.

Ellen appeared in a blue cotton gown that reached mid-calf with broad shoulder straps that buttoned in front. It was the first time he'd seen her shoulders bare. They were squarish even without pads, but there was nothing masculine about them. Her hair glistened like poured gold. She stooped a little, embarrassed by her height—she was five-eight, thereabouts—and her smile was guarded.

He breathed. "You look like Carole Lombard."

"She's dead," said Ann. He could learn to hate her.

But Ellen ignored her—from practice, he suspected. "You look like Jacob Heppleman, only handsomer. You were made for a dinner jacket."

"He said he felt like Count Dracula."

Ellen said, "Aren't you late for your concert?"

"Holy shit!" Ann looked at her watch, strapped on the underside of her wrist. She gulped her drink, got up, snatched a fur-trimmed stole and a pillbox hat from a rack, and waggled five scarlet nails at them on her way out.

"Anyway," said Ellen, "she's housebroken."

He laughed, full out and loud.

"If she's in mourning, I'm Eleanor Roosevelt."

Her gaze was frank. "Her dear old dad was a long-haul trucker. Turned out he had another wife and two kids in Iowa. She didn't know until they showed up at the funeral."

"She didn't waste any time getting cynical."

"Oh, she was always like that. Now she has an excuse. Is that for me?" She pointed at the box on the table.

He'd forgotten all about it. He picked it up. "This was the custom when I shipped out. You don't have to wear it."

She accepted the box, drew off the bow, and tore away the wrapping. The gardenia let out a puff of scent when she lifted off the top. She removed it. "Do the honors?"

He took it with an unsteady hand. The pin looked wicked. "Are you sure it's worth a purple heart?"

"Jacob. It's only going to be 1946 four more hours. Do you want me wearing last year's corsage?" She closed in and placed it in his hand, cupping both of hers around it.

———

Les Brown and His Band of Renown was playing at the Plaza. Doris Day, twenty-four years old in a liquid-silver gown, sang "Sentimental Journey" just the way it should be sung once everyone had made the journey back home. They slow-danced, Jacob's slightly moist hand gripping Ellen's cool dry one, the other on the small of her back.

She tilted her head to meet his eyes. "Where'd you learn to dance?"

"Did I step on your toes? I'm sorry. Too many forced marches. My calluses have calluses."

"I meant you dance well. Answer the question."

"USO."

"Oh."

"Disappointed?"

"A little. I thought it might have been some jade in a Paris brothel."

"Everyone has such romantic notions of my service. I never got within a hundred miles of the Eiffel Tower."

She lowered her head to his chest and they danced a few bars without speaking.

"You didn't ask me where *I* learned." Her voice vibrated through his sternum.

"I thought girls were born knowing how."

"For a writer, you don't know much, do you?"

"I'm beginning to find out how much I don't."

The conversation was threatening to become intimate. She changed the subject, as if she'd sensed possible tension. "How's the great American novel coming along?"

"Thank you for not applying pressure."

"Sorry. We agreed I'm not a writer. We ordinary folk don't know what we should and shouldn't say."

"You're not ordinary. It's one of those things; like Ann calling me Shakespeare. We hacks hate that."

"You're not a hack. And I told you not to pay any attention to her."

He wanted to ask about the other thing Ann had said, about Ellen having lost the love of her life to the service. "I'm curious about how you became friends."

"She answered my ad for a roommate to share expenses. I didn't feel one way or the other about her until she ponied up her half of the first month's rent right on time. After that she was the sister I never had. Why don't you want to talk about your book?"

He'd told her Robin Elk's idea for *The Fence*.

"There's nothing to talk about. My source keeps teasing me with all the shady contacts he has, but he won't say who they are or where I can find them." He filled her in on Pickering, leaving out how they'd met. He didn't think he'd ever know her well enough to share that story.

"Do you really need those contacts? They sound dangerous. What if they think you're a snitch?"

"'Snitch'? You've been reading too much Heppleman. I wouldn't pump them like Boston Blackie. I'd go in as a customer, pawn my good conduct medal or something, look around, get the feel of the place."

"Wouldn't it look and feel like Pickering's?"

"I won't know that until I get inside one."

"What's the matter with using your imagination?"

"Pickering said pretty much the same thing. Civilians don't understand."

"This one doesn't."

"I can't write about a fence without ever having met one in the flesh. It's like war. You can read what all the experienced people have to write about it, try to imitate them, maybe even fool some people who've never seen it, but until you've been there yourself you don't know the first thing about it."

"You got out alive. Aren't you pushing your luck?"

He leaned back to look down at her. "Are you really worried about me?"

The song ended, sparing her the necessity of answering the question, which he'd already regretted asking; peacetime was a minefield that no one had charted for him. The dancers applauded. They returned to their table as the band struck up "My Dreams Are Getting Better All the Time."

His Scotch was tepid, the ice cubes floating shapelessly on top like dumplings. He ordered another and a fresh vodka-tonic for Ellen.

"How's the job search?" he asked while they waited.

"I've got an interview next week, at a brokerage firm downtown. Seems they're having trouble finding someone who can type, take dictation, do arithmetic, and spot-weld a B-29. I'll probably be doing a lot more of the first three."

"How's class?"

"Over and done with. I finished with a *B*."

"Been an *A* if you played ball with Tharp."

"What do grades mean in the real world?"

"Maybe nothing. Something, maybe. It's not the same world they ordered me to save. I don't know what it is yet, but it isn't the same."

Their drinks came. Her eyes reflected the sparkle in her glass. "That's good. You should write that."

"I'm pretty sure a thousand other guys are doing just that. My agent says we ex-G.I.'s are a drug on the market."

"And what was your agent doing while you were away fighting for flag and country?"

"Sitting tight, making money hand over fist. Not very patriotic, but it means he knows what he's talking about. So instead of the world, I'm going to write about people who deal in hot merchandise."

"Selling yourself short, Heppleman."

"Holly. Jack Holly."

She wrinkled her nose. "Sounds like a vaudeville comic."

He was only half listening. The music was muted, the figures on the dance floor a distant blur.

"What if those people's world *is* the world as it is now?" he said.

"I don't get you."

"Me neither." He rose. "Let's dance."

She stayed put. "Why are you changing the subject?"

"When you get an idea you don't smother it by thinking about it."

An hour and a half later, they pressed themselves into the crowd in Times Square. Snow fell among premature scraps of confetti, the flakes frozen hard as steel shavings by the sub-freezing air; but the close-packed celebrants, wrapped in overcoats, each contributing 98.6 degrees of body heat, warmed the space between the canyon walls like steam rising from an outdoor sauna. When the ball began its jerky, pulley-driven descent from the top of the Times Tower, 1947 in electric lights blinking off and on at the summit, thousands of cheering throats and dozens of orchestras playing "Auld Lang Syne" created an ear-shattering vacuum of air like the Hiroshima bomb. Jacob and Ellen could barely move in the crush, but they wrapped their arms around each other and kissed with the violent desperation of a couple about to be separated by war.

CHAPTER
FOURTEEN

"The '42 Chardonnay, I think, Jeffrey. It's chilled?" Robin Elk lifted his eyebrows at the Jamaican waiter in scarlet cutaway and white shirt, waistcoat, and breeches, reminiscent—not entirely by accident, thought Jacob—of an eighteenth-century British Army uniform.

A white-gloved hand took the menu Elk had filled out. "Since seven this morning, sir; before we opened."

"Splendid."

The publisher and his guest were seated in the dining room of the Staghunters Club, whose membership was made up chiefly of British subjects of a certain class living in New York. Elk had translated the Latin motto that accompanied the coat-of-arms in the foyer, a caricature of a swollen John Bull standing with one foot on the throat of a rat-faced minuteman: "Even in exile, we are victorious."

"A gesture of colossal insecurity," he added in an apologetic tone. "The drawing is after Cruikshank, trumpeting the burning of Washington during the 1812 war. Supply lines are long, and Yankee pot roast is far superior to beef Wellington. Some chaps can't get past that."

"I'm glad you said that. I was thinking of getting together with my buddies from the service to kick your butts for the third time." He constructed his most charming smile, to draw the fangs from the remark.

He wasn't entirely successful. Elk's smile was wintry.

"Indeed. Well, thank God recent events have put an end to all that. Someone's always crying to take down that monstrosity;

but I'm afraid we're stuck with it as long as a founding member yet breathes who remembers the Boer War."

The building was a relic of old New York: Four stories of pink sandstone with corners rounded by the elements and windows with blown-glass panes offering a bulbous view of Lower Manhattan like a picture taken with a fish-eye lens. They'd passed through a reading room redolent of old leather and tobacco, books on walls and newspapers strewn on tables, the publisher leaning slightly on his cane, his feet shod in shapeless moccasins, and sat down at a small square table draped in crisp linen. This room contained a dozen others under a high coffered ceiling inside walls of English walnut. The moth-eaten head of a stag with mythic antlers glared glassily at Jacob. A monocle would not have seemed out of place.

"Suffocatingly English, Yes? Yes." For a senior executive, Elk was unusually sensitive to the internal musings of companions. "And absurdly spot-on, like your American murder mystery films set in England, with a gun room in every house and the daily fox hunt. We use tea bags now—marvelous invention, and sure evidence of the rise of the Columbian Empire—and we can't get enough of John Wayne. Had he been at Munich in '38, we'd have had no need for Churchill. No reflection on Winston. My father hopes to publish his memoirs now he has time on his hands."

"I can't think why he was voted out of office."

"It's the old case of the working mastiff versus the fighting bull terrier, like your man Patton. There simply was no place for him in peacetime. But we're talking about the war once again. Here is Jeffrey, come to our rescue."

The waiter, all articulated bone beneath *café au lait* skin, balanced his tray on one hand and set out their food and wine. Jacob studied his shellfish, fanned out in thin shingled slices on a bed of pink horseradish sauce: *Uncle Haiyam, forgive me; I don't keep kosher.*

Elk, for once, misinterpreted his reaction. "A tough fish, as some might persuade you. Here, however, the chef's burly assistants beat it with mallets and whatnot until it runs up the white flag like"—he glanced around and dropped his voice to a whisper—"General Cornwallis. It's silken to the palate."

He nodded—appreciatively, he hoped. Five years of Spam and powdered eggs had left him indifferent to food.

Still, the abalone was everything his host said it was and the greens and dessert worthy of the surroundings.

The incomparable Jeffrey brought a selection of cigars banded in red and gold foil. Jacob declined. Elk chose one carefully, after passing the first two below his nostrils and rustling them next to an ear. The waiter ignited it with a gold lighter and withdrew.

It all seemed so well rehearsed it left the observer with an inflated sense of his own importance, as if it had been performed for him alone. *Come off it, Jake, m'boy; you're just another horse in the stable.*

"I asked you here," Elk said at last, "outside the formal confines of the office, because I sense you're troubled. I've yet to see pages, and I know from your history you're no laggard. Is it the dreaded Block?"

"I wish everyone wouldn't use that word as if it were capitalized, like the Plague. It gives it a gravity it doesn't deserve. I've never heard of a plumber's block. It's just a fancy phrase for laziness."

"I fail to see the comparison. A plumber looks at a leaky pipe or a stopped drain, identifies the source of the problem, and attends to it. Artists require inspiration."

"Inspiration's cheap. Any child can tell an elaborate lie and get out of a spanking."

"What motivates you?"

"Rent."

Elk's smile was almost broad. "Capital answer! I was prepared to sit through a lecture on art and significance. More than ever

I'm convinced I was right in selecting you to lead our line. Which is why I'm concerned."

"I'm stuck, that's all. It's not psychological. My research source has been uncooperative."

"If it's a question of money, I may be able to shake something loose from the discretionary fund."

"That's arranged. Anyway, he's not poor, just wary. He has reasons not to trust me that I won't go into."

"You're certain you need him?"

"Yes."

"How can I help?"

"You can't; unless you have connections to the underworld."

Jeffrey came to clear the table. When they were alone, Elk produced a crocodile notebook and a fat green fountain pen. He began writing. Jacob stared.

"This is the address of our best illustrator, Phil Scarpetti." Elk tore off the sheet and gave it to him. "He lives and works in a loft in the lowest part of the Village—and you thought *I* was a cliché. He's doing the cover for *The Fence*; we hope. He's in the way of being a genius, but we overlook that because he's never missed a deadline and his covers sell more books than the bylines. We'd sack the rest of the staff and use him exclusively, except he's temperamental. He accepts only those assignments that appeal to him. He's turned down Saroyan and Aldous Huxley; 'derivative,' he called them. Yes, he actually reads the books we send him. I think you'll benefit from his acquaintance."

Jacob looked at the sheet. It was just a name, a number, and a street. "'Temperamental' usually means pain-in-the-neck."

"Oh, he is. Our first art director resigned rather than work with him again. Went into the seminary."

"I told you I'm not looking for inspiration. If I were, do you think I'd find it in some artist's idea of what I'm going to write before it's written? Most of the time they don't get it right even after."

"I'm not suggesting a pep talk." Elk broke a half-inch of cigar ash into a heavy silver tray. "Scarpetti's an ex-convict, on parole from a ten-year sentence for armed robbery. He may be in a position to put you onto the people you seek."

CHAPTER
FIFTEEN

Phil Scarpetti wasn't listed in the Manhattan directory, which delayed Jacob's decision to make contact. He didn't like drop-ins, much less being one, and based on Elk's comments about the artist's personality, he doubted he'd be turned away with anything approaching politeness.

He was more afraid of his own reaction. In his youth, he had accepted social slights peacefully ("taken shit," in barracks lingo). He no longer knew that person. The incident that first time in Pickering's pawnshop had made him aware of something inside him, something disturbing that might come to the surface suddenly and without warning. The army spent six weeks training a man to act on reflex, without thinking, and no time at all retraining him to use his brain when the crisis was over.

For all his show of British understatement, Elk wasn't subtle. The day after their lunch, a special-delivery package came containing color reproductions of Scarpetti's cover paintings: Plainly the publisher didn't want him to forget his advice to pump the ex-convict for dirt.

Here was the standard paperback palette of bright primaries, the brute imagery. But the brushstrokes were savage: raw slashes, with scant concern for composition or perspective. And unlike the work of other Blue Devil artists, the faces and figures weren't stamped from a mold. They looked like flesh-and-blood types you saw on the street, each unique. Real people, caught in moments of naked emotion: pain, lust, hate, terror. The images approached vivisection.

There was one Jacob kept staring at: A man in his underwear, sitting on the edge of a mattress in a dingy hotel room, a pistol dangling from his hand between bare knees, a woman in a slip sprawled dead at his feet. His face buried in his other hand expressed a depth of despair beyond imagining.

This was no marketing tool. It was a purge.

Damn Elk, anyway. He had to seek Scarpetti out, if only to catch a glimpse of the animal in its cage.

The bus carried him away from twentieth-century New York, letting him off in the collapsed and twisted spinal column of old New Amsterdam, where streets doubled back on themselves, running parallel and perpendicular at the same time, with tiny unexpected parks scattered like divots, each equipped with its anonymous equestrian statue. Armed with a tourist's map from the bus station, he wandered streets barely wide enough to admit a rickshaw, almost colliding with an old woman pushing a cart loaded with piles of steaming onion-smelling dough, and asked for directions three times, until he stood in front of a block warehouse with bricked-in windows and a bay door secured with a padlock. The address, spray-painted on cement, was the one Elk had given him. He turned two corners before he found an unsealed door. When no one answered his knocks he tried the pitted brass knob. It turned and the door opened on freshly oiled hinges—an encouraging sign of life beyond.

"Watch it, brother! You want to lose an eye?"

He froze, his hand still on the knob. The voice, middle-register masculine, caromed off the walls long after it finished. After bright sunshine on snow, the interior was dark as a cave.

"Fire in the hole!"

There was a flash, a sharp *crack* followed by a wet smack, and a blinding burst of color. Jacob hit the dirt from instinct.

His ears were still ringing when the man spoke again. "Sorry about that, soldier. You never know what you're barging into this deep in the Village."

He rose and brushed off dust. His eyes had adjusted. The room was vast. At the far end stood an eight-foot slab of stretched canvas, propped up like a flat on a stage set. A sheet, stained many colors, curtained it on either side. A splotch of violent red and yellow splattered the canvas, running down in rivulets and pooling on the drop cloth at the base. It looked like an evil blossom. On the floor just this side of it slumped the remains of what looked like an army knapsack, burst and smoldering; the odor of scorched cloth filled the room. Wires ran from inside the sack to a two-by-four construction in a corner, braced like a railroad barricade. A man stepped out from behind it, wearing a filthy smock and welder's goggles. He carried a demolition box with a plunger handle. The wires were attached to terminals fixed to the sides.

Just as he made his appearance, the nibbling flame found something it liked inside the knapsack and flared up two feet, pouring black smoke into the rafters. Hurriedly, the man in the smock traded the box for a copper-and-brass fire extinguisher, trotted over, and snuffed out the blaze with a whoosh. The chemical stench was suffocating.

"Can't be too careful. Sometimes a charge goes off late. I lost a week's work last time, and almost an arm."

Jacob studied the man, but could make out nothing beyond blank lenses and shapeless cotton. "How'd you know I was a soldier?"

"If you don't want people to know, next time don't dive. Most people straighten up and clap their hands over their ears. But then, most people knock first."

"I did. Three times."

"Shit, I forgot." He set down the extinguisher and pulled two inches of cotton batting out of each ear. "I thought you were a mumbler."

"Are you Scarpetti?"

"Who the hell else did you expect to find in this dump? And who the hell are you?"

"Jacob Heppleman."

"Never heard of you."

"Robin Elk gave me your address. He might have mentioned me as Jack Holly."

The goggles went up and down in a nod. "Should've known it was an alias. Name like that, I expected a guy with a diamond on his pinky. I liked *Chinese Checkers*. Wish Elk had gone to me for the cover. Red Cooper loads his brushes like spackle."

"I'm with you. I've seen your work."

Jacob grasped a hand stained indelibly, corded on the back with veins as thick as hydraulic cables. The grip came just short of punishing. Scarpetti stood just medium height; he looked taller at a distance. When he took off the goggles, they left a perfect mask of clean olive-colored flesh inside a palimpsest of paint. His hair was cut in a flattop, marine style. He had a rectangular face with high cheekbones and a mitered chin; everything about him was square and sharp, like one of those drafting knives with a blade you broke off in sections to get to a fresh edge. Straight lips and good teeth in a smile that didn't look as if it came cheap. Jacob put him at thirty, although he might skew younger after a good scrubbing.

He found the face familiar. In a flash he knew why. It belonged to all the men in Scarpetti's paintings. The superficial things— hair, coloring, expression—that had made each appear unique were an illusion; a disguise to obscure the fact that the artist served as his own model.

Jacob realized he was staring. He gestured at the canvas.

"I didn't figure you for abstraction."

"Horseshit. You have to be half-mad to be a genius like Picasso, and I've got paying work due tomorrow. Geniuses don't work on the clock."

"Elk thinks you're a genius."

"Dimbulbs generally do. Hank Stratton's got a bank robber blowing himself up in his next, with a dynamite belt gone wrong. I'm trying for the effect of blood, bones, entrails, and fire all going up in one big splat."

"You're right. It's horseshit."

Scarpetti's mouth fell open. Then the good teeth met in a grin. "*Damn!* I knew I liked you the minute you hit the deck. You can't fake real. This is a shortcut, and it stinks. I was sure when I read your stuff you were an artist."

"I can't draw a straight line with a ruler. But for weeks now everyone's been telling me to fake it and no one will know the difference. *I* would. Could you hang a picture you knew something was wrong with on your own wall and live with it?"

Scarpetti met this with no expression at all; a talent Jacob envied. It would have saved him a bundle at poker.

"Are you a drinking man?" the artist said. "Just say you are, even if you throw it in a potted plant. I've been saving a bottle of grappa that drunken prick Hemingway gave me when I told him to take his war novel and shove it up his ass: for my wedding, I thought. Only the bitch ran off with a guy that sells pink flamingos."

"I'm a drinking man," Jacob said. "And I don't see a plant in the joint."

CHAPTER SIXTEEN

The living area was in a loft at the top of an open flight of stairs only slightly less steep than a ladder. An icebox, a chipped enamel sink, and a pump-up gas stove shared the space with a tired armchair and a bed on an iron frame. Bricks had been removed from a window extending below the floor to let in light; old mortar hammocked the corners of the panes like snow. A fluorescent ring shed pale illumination on brown linoleum. The place smelled of stale grease and mineral spirits.

Scarpetti swung open the oven door on squawking hinges and removed a fat jug that at one time might have contained bleach. New York bachelors never baked, it seemed.

At least Jacob assumed his host had stayed single after the pink-flamingo episode. The female touch was patently absent. A paint-streaked wooden stepladder made a drying rack for an odd number of socks.

"I don't know how long I'll be able to stay on here." Scarpetti filled a pair of mismatched glasses with clear liquid from the jug. He'd shed his smock, which had been only partially successful in protecting his flannel shirt and dungarees from spatters. "I only pay rent on the loft. The owner lets me use the rest of the place as a studio, but he wants to put in apartments as soon as he can get his hands on the material. The war slowed everything up."

"Did you serve?"

"They don't take convicted felons." His tone was the same as if he'd said he had flat feet.

Jacob accepted a glass and toured the space. Finished canvases hung unframed on bare brick and leaned against it in stacks. He recognized the originals of the prints Elk had sent, among startling new scenes of cigarette-smoking teenagers lounging in alley doorways, beetle-browed army sergeants encircling an undernourished private in a barracks, a woman caught in broad daylight wearing makeup intended for a neon-lit bar, looking like a pathetic clown abandoned by the circus. In every picture, it seemed as if something violent had just happened or was just about to.

"I've seen some of these places around town. Do you paint on location?"

"Sketch. Set up an easel anywhere in this burg and in two minutes you've got a crowd. I can't stand people looking over my shoulder when I work."

"Models?"

"Paint 'em in later. Pay 'em out of my fees. Elk runs his shop on the cheap, using the same models over and over. That's why all Blue Devil covers look alike. The Chinese girl on *Chinese Checkers* is a Filipino spy on *Mindanao Massacre* and a Japanese masseuse on *Tokyo Nights*."

This coming from a man who painted himself almost exclusively; but Jacob resisted saying it. "You can't have much left after paying your own models."

"I don't use professionals. They all come with the same stock poses. Getting 'em to break out is like trying to coax a milk horse off its route. Give me a file clerk or a gypsy cab driver. Does that look graceful to you?" He pointed his glass at a woman shrinking away from a man's raised hand on the floor of a dime-a-dance club. Her lipstick was smeared, her eyes wide, like a wild animal's.

"Not at all."

"A pro would've done *Camille*. When it comes to a woman taking a beating, the awkwarder the better. All I had to tell her was what was going on. You just know she's been there. I found her slinging drinks in a dive on Twenty-Second."

"When I saw you I thought they were self-portraits."

"The men, you mean."

Odd thing to say.

He rolled a shoulder. "There's a piece of me in all of 'em. Isn't there some of you in the people you write?"

"Sure. You spend a lot of time scouting prospects."

"Not really. It's like deer hunting. Pick your spot, sit down, and sooner or later one walks right up to you. Sometimes it's pure accident. I was browsing for neckties in Macy's when I found that palooka there, the one in his BVDs with the dead blonde. Selling men's cologne."

"He doesn't look like it."

"That was the idea."

Jacob sipped his drink. It took his breath away. It was pure grain alcohol, a step removed from the paint thinner he was breathing. "What *is* grappa, anyway?"

"It's made from the skins and stems left over after they crush the grapes. Hemingway practically lived on it in Spain. It's cheaper than gin. Makes a terrific aftershave." Scarpetti climbed onto the bed, propping himself up with pillows. The springs brayed. "Elk said to expect you. He thinks I know everybody on the wrong side of the tracks from Frank Costello on down."

"Did he say why I wanted to see you?"

"He told me about *The Fence*. Swell idea. Don't know why nobody's done it already. You don't know any fences?"

"He said I should wing it."

"The dope. Without a true bill your pet crook would look like Clark Gable and talk like David Niven. And I wouldn't be doing the cover."

Jacob sat in the chair. He sank down until his knees were higher than his waist. The grappa was beginning to take effect. The heat climbed his ribs and burned his ears. He got bold. "Did you really pull a stick-up?"

Scarpetti took cigarettes and matches from his shirt pocket, offered the pack. Jacob shook his head. The artist lit one for himself. "I was a stupid kid. I read a piece about Dillinger in

Liberty, stole a pint of Four Roses from a drugstore, drank it all in the alley, and went back in waving a Boy Scout knife. Cops were already there. The druggist called them after I swiped the liquor."

"Elk said you got ten years. Kind of stiff for a kid his first time out."

"Who said it was my first?"

He dodged that one. "Did you study art in prison?"

"A guy on my block taught it in junior high till the janitor caught him with a girl in the seventh grade. I started out drawing oranges and boxes on the floor by my bunk; by the time I got sprung I was painting the warden's portrait in oils. You can trade with the guards for almost anything but a nude model." He grinned. "Yeah, I asked."

"What was your first professional job?"

"Pen-and-ink illo for *Silk Sheets*. The art director liked the way I draw tits. Those porno rags could afford to hire nudes."

Jacob liked Scarpetti. He hadn't expected to like anyone in the paperback jungle. "How come you still know underworld characters?"

"See, that's why you need me. You say 'underworld' around these gorillas, they'll feed you to the rats. Why *shouldn't* I know them? Not all my models came from Macy's."

"Fence shops?"

"Fence shops, flophouses; a newsstand on Tenth Avenue where the black market boys hang out looking for tips. I learned enough in stir to give 'em the office."

"What if they find out you're sharing their secrets?"

"Well, if you tell on me, it'll make Elk awful mad. If I'm in the river he'll have to use his hacks exclusive."

"Why risk your neck for me? We just met."

"I like the fence idea. And I don't want to spend the rest of my life dressing up Hank Stratton's rotten private eye stories. Listen, you write this the way you wrote *Chinese Checkers*, I'll make you a cover they could hang in the Louvre. If Elk holds up his end, you'll blast Lash Logan out of every barbershop in the country."

"I wouldn't enjoy it if the art's posthumous."

"Don't worry; I'm no Baby LeRoy." He looked at a strap watch. "Help yourself to the vino while I go make a call. I don't keep a phone in the house. The damn things always ring when I'm painting a nostril. Nostrils, that's the secret. Get one wrong, you turn Rita Hayworth into Boris Karloff. My answering service is a bartender down the street." He threw on a paint-stained cotton jacket Jacob had thought was a drop cloth and went out the door.

Jacob didn't pour any more wine. He wasn't really much for drink. He got up to clear the fog, studying the paintings. The man was too good for this racket.

He toured an arsenal of painters' props: blackjacks, pistols, assorted daggers, a bullwhip. He recognized some of the items from Scarpetti's covers. A pipe rack contained chalk-striped suits, low-cut dresses, and lacy lingerie. A clothes tree was a haberdashery of fedoras, cloches, straw boaters, women's evening headgear clustered with feathers and sequins. Tawdry costume jewelry spilled from a dresser drawer. After this, a visit to a genuine fencing operation might prove a disappointment.

He found a shabby black portfolio and spread it open on the bed. He was snooping now. It was packed with charcoal sketches on coarse paper, signed with smudged fingerprints: male and female nudes, landscapes, the Central Park pedestrian tunnel, details of hands and feet, a caricature he recognized immediately as Hedda Hopper. The more serious studies bore no resemblance to the subjects Scarpetti used in his cover art: The female nudes were middle-aged and paunchy, the males anti-heroic, with homely or ordinary features and little muscle definition. One of the women was several months pregnant.

"You found my doodles."

He jumped. Scarpetti had made no noise re-entering. Jacob slapped the portfolio shut and turned.

"Sorry. I'm a nosy jerk."

"Forget it. I'm just glad you didn't find my opium pipe." Scarpetti poured himself another drink. "I wanted to study in Paris, but it kept changing hands. I'd go now, only I can't take the time. I'm too damn successful for my own good." He sat on the bed. "You're all set. Saturday night, six o'clock, one-eleven East Fourth."

"Rough neighborhood."

"You won't find what you're looking for on Park Avenue. Saturday's when Irish Mickey drops in to see how much his people are stealing from him. You don't want to miss him."

"Irish Mickey's your fence?"

"Mickey Shannon. The name he raced under, anyway. Back then, the owners liked their liquor from Kentucky and their jockeys from County Cork. His real name's Isidore Muntz. Don't tell him I said that. His fuse is even shorter than he is."

"It's walking distance, isn't it?"

"Only if you know the Village. There are tourists from the '39 World's Fair still wandering around lost."

"I work not far from there. I know my way home and that's about it."

"The layout makes sense, if you drink as much as the Dutchmen who drew it up. Come back five-thirty Saturday and we'll go meet some crooks."

CHAPTER
SEVENTEEN

He'd invited Ellen to his apartment that night. He spent the afternoon with a mop, carpet sweeper, dustcloth, and Sani-Flush, removing the top layer of bachelor living from a room that, when it came time to make it presentable, suddenly seemed much larger than it was.

Browsing in Woolworth's for something to spruce up the place, he'd bought tea towels. What they had to do with tea he had no idea, but they were only ninety-eight cents for a package of two, and since he wasn't serving tea anyway he hung one next to the sink and the other on the handle of the oven door, but the blue stenciled design of a stylized vase of flowers only made the ivory linoleum floor look dingy and the white sink and stove stark, like fixtures in a morgue. He shut the towels away in a drawer.

He'd planned to cook—in tandem with Campbell's and Chef Boyardee—but the housecleaning took longer than planned, so he overcame past trauma and ordered Chinese.

It arrived in time, brought by a Negro deliveryman wearing a bomber jacket over his apron and a fleece-lined cap with flaps. Jacob took the big paper sack, paid and tipped him, and finished transferring the courses from cardboard to crockery just as another knock came.

He turned on the phonograph, set the needle on a Fritz Kreisler record, and went to the door.

"Something smells delicious. Have you been holding out on me? You're a chef?"

"Me and Madam Ying. Can you handle chopsticks?"

"On the piano or at the table?"

"Maybe we'd better stick to forks and spoons."

"No, let's be adventurous." She removed her hat and shook loose her hair, transforming the apartment in a flash. The tea towels had never been necessary.

He helped her out of her coat. She wore a blue woolen dress that clung to her (Hurrah, static!) and a scent that reminded him vaguely of something lost. "You look great."

"I look like Tugboat Annie. I've been bent over a desk all day under a twenty-five watt bulb. I've got bags under my eyes and a stiff neck."

"May I be of service?" He held up his hands and wiggled his fingers.

She hesitated. "You weren't one of those commandos who killed Nazis with their bare hands, were you?"

"I wore gloves."

She sat in a straight chair while he stood behind her, kneading out the knots where her neck curved into her shoulders. Her skin was so smooth he was conscious of his calluses. Her head swayed with the undulating pressure and she made little contented humming noises.

"So you got the job at the brokerage," he said.

"Today was my first day. I'm sorry I didn't tell you. They called yesterday. I just had time to buy a couple of outfits. You can't start a job in the suit you wore to the interview. I tapped out my checking account, but they pay next week."

"How's your boss?"

"Okay. He's got a fat wife and six really ugly kids in frames on his desk. No roving eye, thank God. I'm not so sure of one of his floor men."

"What's a floor man?"

"A guy who stands on the floor of the stock exchange and yells at the blackboard. He's got a little wispy moustache like Doug Fairbanks and a pot belly. But he's out of the office a lot, so I don't have to pack iron all the time. Golly, that feels good. Learn this in the army?"

"Actually, this is my first time."

"You're a natural. Throw over this writing thing and come work for me."

They were drifting into harm's way. He let go of her neck.

"Let's dig in."

She got up, rotating her neck. "That's so much better."

The violin had finished playing. He switched off the phonograph.

"What a beautiful typewriter."

She was standing in front of a battered metal stand someone had put out with the trash. He'd moved the Remington there from the table.

"All I need's something to write on it." He drew out her chair. She sat, watched him set out the bowls and dishes and slip the chopsticks from their paper sleeves.

"Care to talk about it?"

"After I eat." He had to put something on top of the grappa.

They took a crack at the chopsticks. She was more successful, but when the placemats began to look like Phil Scarpetti's paint rags, they switched to flatware. The food tasted better than it smelled in *The Greenwich Clock*.

He told her about his visit with the artist and the appointment they'd made.

"Irish Mickey Shannon, really? Is he as dangerous as he sounds?"

"Not when you consider his real name's Isidore Muntz."

She frowned. "I think you should give this one a pass. Write about something you know."

"I tried that. Nobody wanted it."

"So write about writing."

He made a snoring noise.

"Jakey, just don't go, okay?"

"I like it when you call me Jakey."

"Don't think I don't notice when you try to change the subject."

"I'm all grown up, Ell. I think I can handle a sawed-off runt with a trick name."

"You didn't grow up in this town. You go there, I never hear from you, how do I know you're not swimming in the East River?"

"What's this obsession everyone has with the river? Doesn't the Mob have any imagination at all?"

"You're changing the subject again!"

They had their first quarrel. It was heated. Forty-five minutes after she arrived, he helped her into her coat without a word and she was gone, no good-bye.

"Oy," he told the closed door.

Ten minutes later came another knock. He was scraping the dishes into the trash. He opened the door. She came in fast, knocking the knob from his hand, and kissed him so hard his lip was still swollen the next morning.

It was clumsy, the way it always was the first time. He was all thumbs undoing her buttons and the catch of her bra. She helped him out of his clothes; he tried to get her stockings off at the same time, and they butted heads; they laughed like idiots. In the next moment they weren't laughing at all. They fell into bed in a heap, her teeth prickling his tongue, her nails digging into his shoulder blades, his thigh pressing insistently between hers.

It was over quickly, mortifyingly so for him. But by the time their breathing slowed to normal, he was ready to go again. She made inarticulate noises. They grew louder, and then her breath caught and he felt her shudder as she went over the edge.

Hours later he awoke to find her lying half on top of him, a leg flung across his pelvis, and his arm asleep beneath her shoulder. He left it there rather than disturb her. Let gangrene set in: What was an arm, anyway?

She started awake, lifting herself from his arm. "What time is it?"

His arm was tingling. He shook circulation into his fingers and looked at his watch. "Six-forty."

"Christ! I'll be late for work."

She used the bathroom, hurried into her clothes while he lay on his back watching, hands behind his head.

He got up, put on his robe, and helped her into her coat. At the door she kissed him again, nearly as violently as the first time.

She pulled her face away and took his in both her hands. Her eyes were wide and deep as quarries.

"Please, please, *please* be careful," she said.

He reached up and brushed a stray strand of hair away from her face. "I've got more reason than ever to be."

She left, her scent remaining. She'd smelled less of the perfume she'd put on the night before and more like him, a humid aroma of stale aftershave, heated skin, and sweaty sheets.

Which was a scent he wanted to remember, and not just because he liked to write the world the way it was, as opposed to the way it appeared in books.

CHAPTER
EIGHTEEN

"Ixnay," Scarpetti said. "Ixnay on that."

Jacob was barely inside the studio door when the artist bumped against him—deliberately, he thought; he didn't think him the clumsy type. Before he could react, a hand groped under his coat and jerked the Army .45 from his belt. Scarpetti held it up in front of Jacob's face. His own was tight under a cloth cap that had seen better days, some of them on the heads of the men on his covers.

"You think Mickey's mugs won't pat you down? In twenty minutes you'll be in a garbage scow on your way to Staten Island with a smile under your chin."

"I didn't know. Gangster etiquette is one of the things I hope to learn."

"Just make like Harpo: Keep your mouth shut and let me do the talking." Scarpetti laid the pistol next to a Chase & Sanborn can filled with paintbrushes.

"What about *your* guns?"

The artist spread his paint-stained jacket. He was unarmed. "Phonies. Plugged barrels and busted firing-pins. They're props. I told you my weapon of choice." He tugged it out of a slash pocket, a small clasp knife with a tarnished BSA shield on the handle.

"You stuck up a drugstore with a Boy Scout knife?"

"You'd rather be stabbed with a Bowie?"

"Still—"

"We're not going into the joint to raid it. It's a field trip, for chrissake."

"How much does Irish Mickey know?"

"The truth, Jack."

"Jacob."

"Okay, Jake. A lie detector's got nothing on these boys. You try to fake it, they figure you're phony all around the track. They'll go to work on you with pliers till they get the whole story, if there's time. If not, bon voyage."

"So he knows I'm a writer looking for material."

"How you think I got the invite? Mickey's a runt, but he's got a head big as Roseland. He thinks you're writing his biography."

"Wouldn't that be like signing a confession?"

"Jesus, you're green. You expect him to level with you?"

"Then what's the point?"

"The *point* is you get a face-to-face with the kind of guy you want to write about. You can get your plot from a police blotter. The rest is what makes 'em tick. You're writing a novel, not a summation for the jury."

Jacob looked at the .45 on the table. Scarpetti saw him.

"Brother, you'd never clear leather. Mickey's all blow, but the punks he pays to loiter under the streetlight outside are Rembrandts with a switchblade."

"'Clear leather'?" He cocked an eyebrow.

Scarpetti made a sly grin. He pointed his chin at a new canvas on an easel, an unfinished painting of a gunslinger with Stetson pulled low and hobnail stubbles on his chin. "Cliff Cutter's latest, *Death and Texas*. Elk just swiped him from Dunlap. Come 1950, you'll have to go to the Morgan Library to find a book in hardcover."

━━━━━━

Saturday at twilight, Midtown Manhattan paused for air between quitting time and the crush of Broadway first-nighters. Compared to it, Greenwich Village at that hour resembled an Egyptian bazaar: Shopkeepers moved their marked-down goods to the sidewalk, shell games sprang up on every corner, booksellers displayed their wares on rolling racks, Runyonesque types worked their way through the press, looking for purses to snatch and pockets to pick. A gaunt dauber in a dirty beret leaned against a rottenstone wall with his masterworks on exhibit.

Scarpetti led the way, pausing now and then to critique a painting, open a book, admire a display of knockoff watches on a vagabond's wrist. He was showing off for his companion, but Jacob enjoyed the performance.

At length the guide stopped, waiting for a delivery van to pass, then snapped his umpteenth cigarette butt toward a sewer grate and crossed in the middle of the block. Jacob scurried to catch up.

Ahead of them a squat brownstone made a smoky presence just inside range of a corner lamp. Jacob could smell the place from across the street: a bleak blend of dry rot, fish deep-fried in old grease, and the carcasses of rodents mummifying inside lath-and-plaster walls.

The building was at least as old as Robin Elk's Staghunters Club, but age was the only thing they shared. The windows were opaque with filth and the rusted iron railings leaned precariously away from their footings in the concrete stoop. Plowed snow was piled in brown clots on either side.

Scarpetti bounded onto the stoop, Jacob following, and pushed a button. The bell made a dull thud inside. They waited, their breath foaming in the frigid air. Then light blossomed in a carriage lamp mounted above the door. It struggled through a paper wasp's nest inside the glass.

It was strong enough, apparently, to illuminate the pair standing on the stoop. After a few seconds a series of locks snapped, an equivalent number of bolts grated, and the door came open four inches. A face without feature hovered inside the gap.

"Tell Mickey it's Phil Scraps," said Scarpetti.

The door thumped shut. Another round of silence, then light came on behind narrow gridded glass cutouts in the door and it swung wide.

Jacob followed the artist inside and wiped his feet on a coconut floor mat, scraping away slush and soot. The gatekeeper took shape: a hook-nosed, stoop-shouldered seventy in a rusty black coat buttoned from neck to insteps. He closed the door, leaning his weight against it until it went into its swollen frame, and reversed the process, twisting knobs and sliding bolts with a hand that looked like a bunch of yellow radishes. He wore a yarmulke on the back of his bald head. When he turned and started back into the house, Jacob took a step that direction. Scarpetti touched his arm, stopping him.

"They deliver here."

They stood motionless on warped floorboards in a circle of light surrounded by gloom. It was like crouching near a campfire, listening for animals waiting for the flames to die down before they pounced.

Stop writing melodrama, Heppleman. He said it to himself under his breath, and saw the breath. It was colder inside than out. The building predated central heating.

Boards creaked. There was a staircase nearby, and someone was coming down it.

"Try not to stare," whispered Scarpetti.

A shoe scraped the floor and then a new party came into the light and stopped, facing them.

Jacob stared.

CHAPTER
NINETEEN

He couldn't help it. Having been told that one of the biggest fences in town had been a jockey, he'd expected a small man, but Irish Mickey Shannon in the flesh redefined *small*. Without the obvious lifts in his shoes the man would hardly reach four feet. The built-up crown and broad brim of his fawn Borsalino, turned down on one side like Scarface Al Capone's, only called attention to his tiny stature. He resembled the umbrella in a sissy cocktail.

He wore a double-breasted suit with a loud check, a necktie with a parrot painted on it, a houndstooth coat over his shoulders like a cape, and spectators on his tiny feet. He was a true dwarf, with a full-size head and stumpy arms; the side pockets of his suitcoat were placed high so he could stick his hands in them. His eyes were large and wide-set, his nose a crinkle in the exact center of his face. He had full, purple lips.

Jacob couldn't picture him mounting a horse without someone to give him a boost, much less riding one.

"Phil Scraps." His voice was startlingly deep.

"Irish Mickey," said Scarpetti.

There was an element of ritual in the exchange.

"Jack Holly." Scarpetti tilted his head Jacob's way.

Shannon's hands stayed in his pockets, his gaze fixed straight ahead; if you wanted to make eye contact, you had to stoop. "Scraps says you're a scribbler. What kinda stuff you write?"

"Novels and short stories."

"Why?"

He paused. No one had ever asked him that. "Kill time, I guess."

"Huh. What'd time ever do to you? I'd swap a bundle for the three years I spent in juvie, all for a tin watch."

"If I write about you, somebody else might learn how to tell tin from platinum."

"I should give 'em a break?"

"It could make you famous."

"I *am* famous. They know me clear down to the Battery."

"They could know you clear to San Francisco."

Shannon's eyes slid toward Scarpetti. "This character's got a line of blab."

"I told you he's a writer."

The little man offered his hand then. It fluttered in Jacob's, then returned to its pocket. Jacob said, "Thanks for agreeing to see me, Mr. Shannon."

"Mickey. 'Mr. Shannon' sounds like a nag that ran dead last in Tijuana."

"That's where Mickey got his start," Scarpetti said. "He was too short to compete here. Then the war came along and Detroit hired away all the regulars as riveters, on account of they fit in tight places. The owners weren't so picky then about their jockeys. He came back up here and made his grubstake."

"Just in time, too," said Shannon. I got caught in King-of-Prussia's stall with a Kotex. After the racing commission in Mexico City bounced me I diversified my interests."

"Kotex?"

Shannon touched one of his nostrils. "A horse does all his breathing through his nose. How I got caught, I was taking *out* the hag rag after the race. I left it in, I'd of been clean. But I didn't want to kill a horse just 'cause it's too stupid to open its mouth when its nose don't work. What the hell. The war couldn't last forever, and I had a bellyful of tortillas and marimba bands."

"So how'd you get into this business?"

"Some folks got so much stuff they can't hardly move. Others don't got enough to live. Me, I take up the slack."

"Mickey's a combination Robin Hood and Karl Marx."

The little man glowered at the artist. "I'm no Commie. I take showers and I voted for Willkie." He pointed a thumb at Jacob. "You write about me, I get first look. Otherwise you don't leave the neighborhood." He unbuttoned his suitcoat and spread it, exposing the walnut handle of a semiautomatic pistol in an underarm holster. "I can pick the eye out of a rat at fifty yards."

Jacob nodded. He was glad he'd left the .45 behind.

"Swell." Shannon buttoned the coat. "Getting started was easy. I spent a lot of time in hotels on the circuit, made friends with the help. They got keys to all the rooms and don't get paid shit. But they don't know where to lay off the merch. That's where I come in.

"You meet all kinds hanging around the ten-dollar window: jewelers, salesmen, indies that deal out of car trunks. I split even. Think; half the cops are gone overseas. Business is booming on the black market, and the word's out you get a square deal from Irish Mickey every time. Repeat customers, that's the secret." He shifted his gaze from Jacob's sternum to Scarpetti's. "See, that's capitalism. Joe Stalin wouldn't last a week in this racket."

"I stand corrected."

Jacob was wearing his army greatcoat. He put a hand on the lapel. "May I?"

"Depends on what you're going for."

"Just this." Moving slowly, he opened the coat, drew out *Chinese Checkers,* and held it out. The little man took it, frowned at the cover, turned it over and read the back.

"Sex stuff. I want pussy, I go get it. I don't read a book about somebody else getting pussy."

"It's to let you know Phil didn't misrepresent me."

He opened it to the title page. "What's this?"

"My name. I signed it."

"Nuts. I can't sell a book somebody wrote in." He tossed it into the gloom, where it landed on something other than the floor. But his mood was brighter. He rubbed his hands. "Let's go see what Santa brought."

They followed the little man down a narrow hallway, Shannon flipping wall switches as he went. The place was scarcely less bleak for the light.

They stopped finally in a room that ran the width of the house, with a ten-foot ceiling from which hung fluorescent tubes in metal troughs. Shannon walked through it, tugging chain switches. The tubes fluttered on one by one. Here the light entered every corner.

Jacob felt his jaw drop. The room was stacked with containers— cardboard cartons, wooden packing crates, steel drums, tins, shipping tubes—in rows eight feet high, with aisles running between them lengthwise and crosswise, like streets between skyscrapers. They were stenciled with familiar names: WESTINGHOUSE, MAYTAG, DUMONT, HOTPOINT, BERGDORF GOODMAN, MACY'S, LUCKY STRIKE, OLD MILWAUKEE, PHILCO; so many that after a while the letters began not to make sense, as if written in a foreign language. There were refrigerators, washing machines, TV sets, kitchen ranges, radios, cartons and cartons of cigarettes, cases and cases of beer, silk dresses, Arrow shirts, costume jewelry, men's and women's watches: A city built entirely of merchandise, and all of it apparently stolen.

"This baby here's my retirement." Shannon smacked a palm against an oblong crate that might have contained a coffin. It was stenciled CURTIS MATHES. "Combination radio, record player, and TV. All yours after forty-nine easy payments, unless you know yours truly, who'll give you a sweetheart deal. Buy one of these, you'll never have to take out the little woman again. Can't keep 'em in stock."

The tour continued. A stone lion that might have come from the porch of the New York Public Library roared silently in a crate with openings between the slats. A magician's cabinet stood bare, decorated with stars and harlequins in glitter paint. ("Disappearing act," Mickey said, "right off the stage at the Apollo during the show. I thought when I opened it the magician would still be inside.") A cardboard box with holes in the top marked VIVANT

ENFANTS POUSSINS. Jacob retained just enough French to know it was supposed to contain live baby chicks. He cocked his ears, but heard no cheeping from inside.

Mickey noticed. "French novels. Coast Guard seizes porno at the docks. Livestock goes straight to quarantine. I got people there."

He gestured disparagingly toward a crate he could have stood up in: ROCK-OLA, the label read. It was a jukebox.

"That was a mistake. I was getting my tonsils out and the punk I left in charge bought it off a forklift driver with a bad sense of direction. Frankie Costello's got all the juke routes sewed up clear down to Florida. If I was to try to move this myself, there'll be a yard and a half less of Irish Mickey Shannon in the world."

Scarpetti asked him how much he wanted for it.

"I just got through telling you it ain't for sale."

"I don't plan to make money off it. I can use it as a prop when I'm painting a scene in a gin mill."

"You don't tell nobody where you got it."

"I can't spare a yard and a half of myself any more than you can."

"For you, three-fifty."

"Skip it. I'll bring my sketchbook to a bar."

"Suit yourself. I know one of Costello's boys. I'll make him a present. You can't have too much goodwill."

"Where does all this stuff come from?" Jacob asked.

Mickey smiled. His teeth were the biggest thing about him; his mouth seemed barely to contain them. "It's a crime the way some guys drive trucks. Shit keeps falling off."

"Sometimes at gunpoint," Scarpetti said, *sotto voce*.

Shannon took a fat wallet from his hip. When he opened it, an accordion series of glassine pockets unfolded nearly to his shoes. A rainbow assortment of cards showed. "I pay dues to every union in town, not counting the Policemen's Benevolent Association." He ticked them off, folding each card back into the wallet as he came to it. "Teamsters, stevedores, pipe-fitters,

electricians, switchboard operators, waiters, dishwashers, Lino-
typists, carpenters, hotel clerks, driving instructors, hacks, railroad porters, barbers, manicurists—"

"Manicurists?" Scarpetti grinned.

"Listen, that one was easier to get into than railroad porters.
The high-class coloreds got that one nailed down." He continued. "Stonemasons, bricklayers, housepainters, bookkeepers—
here's my favorite, projectionist. Ann Sheridan's in town, she
wants to screen her latest for her Park Avenue friends, I'm her
man."

Jacob said, "Has that ever happened?"

"I'd settle for Rin Tin Tin. Brewers, mechanics, sanitation.
Stock boys smuggle all kinds of shit into trash bins; spoil your
faith in human nature." He put away the wallet. "These here
affiliations are my biggest investment, also my best. I got a warehouse on the Hudson full of wire and pipe from the electricians'
and plumbers', and I'm charging double now that people are
building houses again."

"What about the police?"

"My second biggest investment. They think I'm a millionaire."

"You *are* a millionaire," Scarpetti said.

Shannon stuck his thumb at Jacob. "You don't write that. I
don't need Internal Revenue snooping around."

"This is all off the record. I'm writing about a garden-variety
fence, not General Motors."

"I didn't start at the top. It's a regular Horace Alger story."

"I'd be accused corrupting our youth. They'd jail me for contributing to the delinquency of minors."

"Unless you kill the guy off," Phil said.

Mickey shuddered. "Cut that out. It's bad luck."

They left the little man and walked back to Scarpetti's loft. It was
snowing, but the flakes dissolved when they reached the sidewalk. The seasons had begun to turn just while they were inside.

"Nobody patted me down," Jacob said. "I didn't even see any henchmen, unless you count Methuselah at the door."

"That was Mickey's Uncle Sid. He keeps him around for luck. I didn't really think you'd get the full treatment. But you never know when a guy's seen too many movies."

He stepped up the pace. "You know, that's not a bad idea, telling Mickey's life story. Change his name, make him life size, and cut him up with a chain saw in the end. I'll order more Cadmium Red."

"No chain saws. I'm not writing a horror comic book."

"You're writing, though, right now. I know that look. I've seen it in the mirror."

"Jack *Holly's* writing. I haven't the slightest idea what Jacob Heppleman's up to."

CHAPTER TWENTY

"You know what today is, don't you?"

———

Oh, dear God.

He decided not to try and bluff his way through. "I'm guessing it's significant. Let's get the fight out of the way so we can make up in the sack."

They were in Ellen's new apartment. She'd moved in a month before. That took roommate Ann out of the equation, with no objection from him. There were still things in cardboard cartons in the living room, which had come furnished in someone else's taste; but the neighborhood was respectable and the building super was an ex-marine, with the protective instincts of a mastiff.

"Silly. I first saw you six months ago today."

Had it been that long? Yep: He'd started writing *The Fence* at the end of January, and now the galley proofs were on his dining room table. "So what'd you think?" he asked.

"Good posture. I had you down for a colonel at least. One of those battlefield promotions, where someone who looks like Tyrone Power storms a machine-gun nest and takes Hitler prisoner, then comes home to sell war bonds."

"I thought I looked like Jimmy Stewart."

"Don't be a goof. You had broad shoulders and lean hips. A cowboy, if not a colonel."

"I've filled out a little since."

"What'd you think of me?"

They were sitting on a red plush sofa that belonged in a shabby hotel lobby, her head on his shoulder.

"Nice legs."

"That's all you remember?"

"You called that instructor—what was his name?"

"Tharp."

"Tharp. You called him a son of a bitch."

"That was you. I called him a shit. So I had nice sticks and a potty mouth. Great first impression."

"Is this the fight?"

"It is if you don't kiss me right away."

That attended to, he said, "I've been meaning to ask you something."

"It's henna rinse. Mouse-brown at the roots."

"I knew that. I've been in your medicine cabinet."

"You snooped?"

"I was doing research."

"So you know all my secrets."

"Not all." He hesitated. "Ann told me you lost the love of your life in the war. I thought you'd been engaged or something and he was killed in action. But you never mentioned it, so—"

"Is it important?"

"I need to know who my rival is so I can compete."

"It's not much of a competition when he's dead."

"It's worse. He's not around to make an ass of himself from time to time so I don't make an ass of myself running down the dear departed."

She leaned away from him and lit a Lucky. "Ann's quite the storyteller. I'm surprised she doesn't write books herself; juicy ones they keep under the counter."

"Look, if it's too painful—"

"It is, and I'd rather not go into it now. Is that okay? I'm not trying to be mysterious."

"Okay."

But it wasn't, and after a few more minutes he left.

Back in his apartment he fixed himself a drink and nursed it for an hour proofing *The Fence*. He hadn't seen galleys since before the war, and had forgotten how pleasant it was to read his own writing in print, when he'd finished second-guessing himself. Now he could concentrate on typos and last-minute bursts of inspiration.

Somewhere on Long Island, a Linotypist had cast Jack Holly's words in lead alloy, then used an ink roller to press the letters onto cheap newsprint, four pages per sheet. In the weeks to come, the corrected copy would be duplicated twenty thousand times on a cylinder press, trimmed, bound, and shipped to every retail outlet in the U.S. that contained a paperback rack. There, some browser might pick it up, intrigued by Phil Scarpetti's arresting artwork, skim the description on the back ("He made his living off the misfortunes of others: until fate—and a blonde named Marcy—made it his dying!"), look at the excerpt on the flyleaf ("'If you won't buy my grandmother's watch, what *can* I sell you?' Marcy implored the fence."), and possibly plunk down two bits to read the rest.

Jacob would never get over the wonder of it; that a grown man should make up stories, write them down, and expect sane people to buy them. It filled him with pride and shame at the same time.

His research had only begun with Irish Mickey Shannon. He'd spent weeks in the Battery interviewing dock workers, in bus stations and truck depots and taxi garages talking to drivers, buying trinkets in Macy's and Gimbels to get salesgirls to open up; plundering the Bronx, Brooklyn, and Queens for authentic color. It was important to get the working class right, because Robin Elk believed it to be Blue Devil's core market.

"Jack Holly's" fence, Mike Moynihan (Good-bye, Herbert Jackdaw), belonged to that world. He was in a hurry to make his fortune, and the first step was to shitcan scruples. He bore little resemblance to Irish Mickey Shannon; not because Jacob feared his displeasure, but because even anti-heroes must be pleasant to look at. Elk was a stickler on that point: "It's women who buy books, Jack; they're the ones who go shopping." Scarpetti's men were slightly battered matinee idols with powerful physiques.

Mike Moynihan starts out desperate. Fresh from the war and broke, he steals a typewriter from a pawnshop hoping to turn it into cash. Caught by the owner, he repents, and moves the kindly old soul (Good-bye, Linus Pickering, hello Father Flanagan type) to take him under his wing and show him the pawnbroking business. But a sudden opportunity to profit from stolen goods leads him deeper and deeper into the black market, and higher and higher on the criminal ladder until he controls most of the contraband traffic in New York.

Jacob had moved Shannon's base of operations to Harlem, partly to shield his source, but also for artistic reasons: No other neighborhood in the city offered so thorough an atmosphere of an alien culture, a world complete unto itself. Jacob had wanted to make his protagonist colored, but Elk vetoed that after reading the early pages: "Sad to relate, old boy, but a Negro in the lead would wipe out the market down South: Piggly Wiggly accounts for fifteen percent of sales there." And so he was reborn shanty Irish.

There was a woman, of course: Marcia "Marcy" Elliott. In the first draft she was Ellen; but that was for his eyes only. In revision he fell back on subterfuge yet again. Women had peculiar notions about broadcasting their private acts to the world.

Marcy was Moynihan's undoing, that was a given from the beginning, when she wandered into his shop, desperate (that word again) to sell her grandmother's gold lapel watch to pay for her mother's (scratch that) father's (scratch that) brother's (scratch that) operation (revise; it was too much like Dickens. Make it dreams of Broadway stardom, reduced to the reality of a coldwater flat on Tenth and the rent two months past due). Moynihan, callous cad, buys her virtue instead. Her revenge comes when she tricks him into buying and selling a stolen jukebox, bringing him to the attention of "Blinky" Fantonetti, the Juke King of Jersey.

On the last page Mike turned the key in the ignition of his Cadillac, and Phil Scarpetti got his explosion: a bonus panel on the back cover, a rare extra outlay on the part of Robin Elk, the Penny-Pinching King of Manhattan.

Raw melodrama, everything but the villain twisting his moustache, dished up without apology. Not *David Copperfield*; not even *Varney the Vampire,* which at least had the virtue of originality; but steps above *Lash Logan, Private Eye.* He was satisfied enough to put the name Holly to it; the pseudonym had by now acquired a legitimacy of its own.

Scarpetti approved. He'd even given him the original art, which hung now unframed on a wall: A dissolute-but-dashing rogue in the foreground, counting crumpled and greasy bills onto the counter of a shop filled with looted treasures, ignoring the blonde disrobing behind him, despite her center spot in the composition. On the book, *THE FENCE* in bulbous yellow letters, *by Jack Holly* in smaller type in white, with the bratty Blue Devil leering in the upper right-hand corner, the size of a penny stamp.

But what to do about Ellen? She'd kept asking to read the book, but he'd put her off, saying it wasn't ready to show. Now here it was in print, the intimate details of their relationship public property.

Then again, she had her own secrets, didn't she?

CHAPTER
TWENTY-ONE

Dear Valued Contributor:

You and a guest are cordially invited to attend a
celebration of Blue Devil Books's new line of
original fiction, to take place
Saturday, June 7, 1947
at 7:30 P.M.
in the offices of Blue Devil Books
16 University Place
New York, NY
Dress casual. Refreshments will be served.
Thank you for joining us in this bold new venture.

Yours most sincerely,
Robin Llewellyn Elk, Esq.

Elk's decision to host the festivities in the publishing house,
with all the doors open to aid the flow, gave the occasion the
air of an office Christmas party. People talked too fast and
laughed too loud, drinks spilled without apology, and someone
had squashed the shrimp from a cocktail into the carpet in Elk's
office like a cigarette butt. Blowups of the covers of the summer
line (was it Jacob's imagination, or was *The Fence* bigger than the
rest, and the half-naked female model's resemblance to Ellen
more pronounced?) hung on every wall and the company mascot
leered down from congratulatory banners printed on Long Island,
blue pitchfork in hand.

"I inquired among the hotels about their banquet facilities, but the pleasant ones were too dear and the least costly looked like a Scarpetti cover," the host told Jacob. "You're not too disappointed, I hope." As was characteristic when he was nervous, he touched his bow tie.

Elk's idea of casual attire was a three-piece suit, blue gabardine, over an Oxford shirt with the collar buttoned down. Today he wore kid-leather slippers on his ruined feet, cunningly designed to look like loafers.

"Not at all," Jacob said. "Those ballrooms are too big and intimidating, and you can't hear what anyone's saying."

"Next year we'll book the Plaza."

He never knew when the Englishman was listening.

Ellen returned from the ladies' room. She wore a blue silk dress with pumps and carried a shiny black clutch. Her eyes were incredibly blue and the ceiling globe in the private office found haloes in her strawberry blond hair.

"This is my friend, Ellen Curry. Ellen, Robin Elk."

Hooking his cane on one arm, he took her hand and executed a smart bow, beaming like the blue devil; in that moment, Jacob recognized a chip off the old block.

"Charming. I see where Jack gets his inspiration."

"I hope that's a compliment. I haven't read the book. I'm not in the habit of disrobing in pawnshops."

"Haven't read it! I hope you don't disapprove of the subject matter."

"How could I? Jacob keeps forgetting to show it to me."

"Artists are absentminded. Fortunately, there is a solution. I wasn't going to distribute these until after the toast; but I'm too weak a creature to make a lovely woman wait." He plucked a glossy red gift bag from a forest of them on his desk. "Cheap trinkets, I'm afraid: perfume for the ladies, aftershave for the men, a shockingly small box of candy, and of course the Product."

The sack contained the items named, including the first ten paperback-original novels ever, tied together with a ribbon—blue, naturally. *The Fence* was on top.

"That's very generous, Mr. Elk."

"Niggardly is the word, madam. As I was telling Jack, better things will come. There's no sense lugging this about all evening. I'll see it leaves with you." He relieved her of the bag. "I must now do myself the injury of leaving your company. Parties don't run themselves."

As Elk mingled, propelling himself with his cane, the young bespectacled man who greeted visitors in the foyer approached with a tray of drinks; he and the pretty blond secretary had been drafted as servers. Jacob, grateful for the interruption, accepted a flute of champagne (domestic, no doubt) while Ellen took a glass of Chardonnay.

"There are celebrities all around you, not that you'd recognize them," he said when the young man left. "I'll introduce you to the ones I've met."

"I can manage, thanks." She opened her clutch and took out *The Fence*. "I'm going to catch up on my reading."

He smiled painfully. "You're a regular Houdini. I didn't even see you untie the ribbon."

"Neither did Elk. He was too busy spreading oil." Her smile was full of mischief. "Go meet the ones you haven't yet." She curled up in one of Elk's leather chairs and opened the book.

He wandered into the press of bodies in the hallway, accompanied by a sense of impending doom.

A hand touched his shoulder. It was Phil Scarpetti, dressed pirate-fashion in an open-necked white shirt with a red scarf loosely tied around his neck. His eyes were muzzy. Jacob's nose told him it was bourbon in his glass.

"Congratulations. It's a hell of a book."

"I'm not sure it's worthy of its cover."

"Can the act. If it's trash, say it. Don't duck your head and stick your toe in the dirt waiting for the world to tell you you're a genius."

Evidently the artist was a belligerent drunk. Jacob switched subjects. "I sent the galleys to Mickey, like he wanted. I never heard back, so I assume he approved."

"You don't assume with that crowd. He might've got it mixed up in a shipment of French pornography."

They were separated by the boil of the crowd. Jacob found himself uncomfortably close to Phoebe Sternwalter, who as P. B. Collier was the only female writer in Elk's stable.

"It's to be our secret," she said, sipping something green from a narrow glass. "According to market research, women tough-guy writers appeal only to lesbians, who apparently don't buy books."

"I liked *Guns at Diablo*."

"My only oater. We've got Cliff Cutter now, so what's the point?"

She was a little wren-like woman in a tweed suit, with steel-rimmed glasses, no makeup, and her hair dragged back in an untidy ponytail. He wondered if she was playing up the lesbian angle, either out of contempt or for her own amusement, or if she was the genuine article.

"Why Collier?" he asked.

"It was Ladies' Day at the Staghunters Club, and *Collier's* was on the magazine table. I could as easily have been P. B. *Saturday Evening Post*."

In Reception he met Burt Woods and Paul Arthur, who as Arthur Burt wrote a cerebral detective series that Elk had snatched from Runson & Sons, an old Boston concern.

"We worked it out scientifically," Woods explained. "'Burt' is second in the alphabet, and customers' eyes start at the top of the rack."

"Why second?" Jacob said. "Why not Burt Arthur?"

Paul Arthur smiled, fingering a curve-stemmed pipe that might or might not have been a prop. "I suggested it; but Burt pecked away until I quit. It's what he does best." Was there just a hint of acid in that Mayfair drawl?

The two men were separate and distinct. Woods was a broad-shouldered Midwesterner with a Henry Fonda accent, wearing a checked flannel shirt and pleated slacks, baggy in the knees. His collaborator was small and narrow in an out-of-season houndstooth suit with patch pockets, round tortoiseshell glasses, and of course the pipe. His speech dripped West End. Woods munched on shrimp the whole time.

"How does it work?" Jacob said. "How do you keep from stepping on each other's toes all the time you're writing?"

"Oh, this is the first time we've been in the same room since we signed the contract," Arthur said. "I mail the plots to Burt, who adds the narrative and dialogue."

Woods swallowed the last shrimp and wiped his hand on his shirt. Jacob guessed then who was responsible for the mess on Elk's carpet. "I'm on the West Coast, and Paul's here. There's barely enough continent for the both of us. We don't exactly get along."

"Quite so. Burt's a shit."

"Paul's what I shit."

Alice, the blond secretary, came up. She'd traded her platter of canapés for a Speed Graphic camera with a flashgun attached. "Hold still, please, gentlemen."

"Arthur Burt" stood shoulder to shoulder smiling while the bulb spent itself with a flare and a plop. Then they sprang apart.

Alice replaced the bulb. "You're my next victim, Mr. Holly. Wait here, please. Cocktail dresses don't come with big enough pockets to carry photo plates." She left.

The lesson of Paul Arthur and Burt Woods wasn't lost on Jacob. For all his show of self-effacement, when Robin Elk cracked the whip, the people who cashed his checks put aside all other considerations.

CHAPTER
TWENTY-TWO

Obediently he remained for a few minutes, until the sniping between Woods and Arthur became too much to bear. He excused himself.

"Jack Holly! Elk pointed you out. Hank Stratton."

A stubby corded paw seized his hand, masticating the bones. Its knuckles were blistered with old scar-tissue.

The author of the Lash Logan, private eye series bore a not-by-a-longshot-accidental resemblance to his creation, albeit shorter and flabbier. He wore a gray fedora that looked as if it had been distressed mechanically, the way car doors were opened and shut thousands of times by a robotic arm at the factory, and an open trench coat (indoors, on a June day that turned asphalt into blackberry jam) over a rumpled brown suit and a black necktie. He had charnel-house breath and gin blossoms on his cheeks.

"Congratulations on your success." Jacob traded his glass for a fresh chilled one from the passing young man and transferred it to his right hand as a poultice against the throbbing. "I hear they're filming *Kill 'em All*."

"Balls. They're shooting the title and using some studio hack's script. It was gonna be in Technicolor and 3D; then the Catholic Decency League put up a stink, so they're shooting it on the cheap on a rented back lot with a nancy TV actor and a Commie director that works cheap 'cause he's blacklisted and using a phony name. They changed Logan to Dugan. Now I hear they want a new title. I'll be lucky if they pay me at all, as why should they? There's nothing left of the book. Say, I read *The Fence*."

"You did?"

"Well, the first chapter. Elk wanted me to give it a blurb."

"Blurb?" It sounded like something in science fiction.

"Puff. Gas. You know, 'I couldn't put it down,' like it was the opposite of a hand grenade. Only I got busy, and then it was too late. I liked what I read. Did the dame shoot him in the end? That's how I'd do it."

"I blew him up. It—"

"Sorry, kid, gotta go. My dame's hungry, and them shrimp don't cut it. Like eating roaches." He gave Jacob a slap on the back that spilled his drink and boated off, the tails of his trench coat flapping.

In a corner languished a young platinum-haired woman in a black sheath and heels that made her tower over Stratton, who hooked her arm and pulled her out the door.

"Beautiful girl. Say what you like about Stratton—and I'll lay odds it's already been said, except 'For He's a Jolly Good Fellow'—he knows where to shop for whores."

Jacob hadn't noticed the speaker, even though he was suddenly aware he'd been standing near for some time. The striking thing about Cliff Cutter, whom he'd met in that same office, was there was nothing striking about him at all. He was a smallish, slight man in his sixties, with close-cut silver hair and a brush moustache only slightly darker. He wore an unobtrusive black suit and held a tumbler filled with an effervescent liquid Jacob suspected was club soda. Nothing about him, including his quiet, almost inaudible speech, indicated he was the author of more than forty rip-roaring western novels. Elk had lured him over from an established hardcover house, beginning with *Death and Texas*, under a deal he was prohibited by his contract with Blue Devil to discuss with anyone.

Which meant it was so lucrative the publisher was afraid all his other writers would demand the same if they knew the figure. Not a bad nest egg for a man who had started out herding cattle in Arizona Territory when Geronimo was still at large. He looked like a shoe clerk.

What Cutter had said sank in. "His date's a private escort?"

Muscles tugged at the corners of the old man's grim mouth. "That's what I like about the East. There's ten names for everything, each one tamer than the last. That's a ten-dollar-a-throw chippie or I'm Sioux City Sue. Only knowing what a dumb cluck Stratton is, she's getting fifty. Man's not a man don't know the value of a dollar or a woman."

"I guess he has it to spend."

"Can't spend it and have it too. I struck pay dirt in '92, went bust, ought-one, went bust, again in 1920, and fell harder that time than all the others. Now I'm rich again, but if there's a God I won't live long enough to turn out my pockets this round. Every time it gets harder to pick yourself back up, and when you do and you're rolling in butter it ain't as much fun as it was."

"Robin says *Pistols West* went back to press twice, and it isn't even officially out yet. That's impressive."

"Would be, if there was a lick of truth in the book. Ever been in a shoot-out?"

"Not if you don't count the war."

"I was, just once. We potted at each other forty-five minutes, counting reloads and ducking around shithouses. Then we both ran out of ammo and all we managed to kill was an afternoon. Ain't had an easy bowel movement since."

"Well, you can't write a western without violence."

"Sure you can. Ever read *Paso Por Aqui*?"

"I can't say I have."

"Jasper named Rhodes wrote it in '25. A hundred and thirty pages without a shot fired or a drop of blood spilt. Dame fine work, and authentic. Didn't sell five hundred copies."

"What was the gunfight about?"

"A mix-up. It wasn't the guy I thought it was."

The small jazz combo Elk had hired for an hour arrived, set up on the landing, and started tuning up. Jacob shook Cutter's hand and passed through another door into a small employee lounge, with cupboards and a counter holding up a huge copper-

and-brass coffee urn and a toaster. At a laminated table sat a plump, pleasant-looking brunette of forty or so in a polka-dot sundress, and a man ten or fifteen years younger in a green suit that shrieked Salvation Army. His hair had been cut by an amateur and his moustache was a smear of ginger.

Jacob never caught their names. The brunette was a chatterbox, the direct opposite of her companion, who never opened his mouth except to insert a pewter flask. The torrent of words from the woman pounded Jacob's ears like a jackhammer. He stole out under the cover of a fresh crowd.

He almost collided with Scarpetti in the hallway. The artist was holding a full glass. His eyes now were red.

"How'd you get on with Brock?" he said.

"Who?"

"Hugh Brock. You were just with him."

"Green Suit? He never introduced himself. *Invisible Aliens* Brock? I heard he was in Hollywood."

"The studio shelved his book. Science fiction hasn't sold a ticket since Flash Gordon. But he's under contract. Thousand a week."

"He can afford better clothes."

"Brock's a queer duck. A buddy that paints sets for Cardinal Pictures told me Brock lives at the Burbank Y, where the silverfish have a standing reservation."

"Who's the woman?"

"His wife, and he married well. She's got the heft to sit on him when he goes off the deep end."

"Drunk?"

"No, that's just his medicine. Every time he shakes his head you can hear screws rattling."

"Veteran?"

"Be a good excuse, but no again. Scuttlebutt is all three military branches rejected him as a schizo. I'm surprised they didn't make him an officer."

"Damnedest party I ever saw." Jacob sipped from his flute, but the champagne had gone flat.

"All it needs is a rabbit with a pocket watch."

"Am *I* normal?"

"Not in this crowd."

He went back to the publisher's office. Ellen sat with *The Fence* shut in her lap, smoking and looking into the middle distance between her and an unknown couple smooching in a dim corner. When she saw him, she put the cigarette out in a large onyx tray filled with butts in her brand, stained with her color of lipstick.

"Marcy Elliott," she said. "Tall, square-shouldered redhead. Why didn't you just use my name?"

He was doubly glad he'd changed it. "You think she's you?"

"Not because of the 'firm ripeness of her breasts.' Jake, there are whole snatches of dialogue that came straight from my mouth."

He glanced nervously toward the couple in the corner.

"Ignore them," she said. "They wouldn't notice if Orson Welles landed with the Martians."

"I borrow from everywhere, Ell. Even *I* don't remember where I got it all."

"Then why haven't I read it before? You're a great writer and a lousy liar. When you said you don't like making things up, I never thought you'd do something like this."

He lowered his voice. "Can we go for a walk? This place is a gossip factory."

"*There* you are!"

He jumped three feet. It was Alice with her camera. "I've been looking all over for you. You promised to stay put. Smile!"

They were startled into smiling. The flash filled his vision with purple and green spots.

"I'm not letting you rush off this time," said the secretary, changing bulbs. "Robin wants all the writers in his office for a group photo."

"Can it wait? We'd like to get some fresh air."

"It'll just take a minute."

He leaned over the desk and touched Ellen's wrist. "Promise you won't leave."

She lit another cigarette. "I'll be here. I'm only halfway through the book." She sat back, opening *The Fence*.

The writers crowded into Elk's office. Jacob found himself standing between Hugh Brock and Phoebe Sternwalter. There was a delay while Alice went to fetch Hank Stratton, who as it turned out had taken his statuesque escort to a drugstore down the street for hamburgers; he came in ruddy-faced and smelling of the common cologne (in that company) of alcohol. As they squeezed in for the shot, Jacob felt Brock flinch. Human contact wasn't his strong suit.

"All together, now, lady and gentlemen," said Robin Elk, leaning on his cane behind the photographer. "Say 'Cheese!' One big happy family."

They obeyed—all except Brock and Cliff Cutter, looking grim as pallbearers—with the blue devil beaming down at them from the banner on the wall.

CHAPTER
TWENTY-THREE

"I want you to understand it isn't making me a slut that I mind."

"Could've fooled me."

They were walking back in the general direction of her apartment. They were in no hurry to catch a cab. It was a warm evening on the cusp of summer and they encountered many strollers under the streetlamps. Jacob and Ellen were carrying their Blue Devil gift bags, like tourists returning to their hotel after a shopping spree.

"Most of your readers won't know where you get your ideas. As for the rest, people who know me know I'm not Marcy."

"Then what—?"

"You hid it from me! It's not just that you didn't trust me to understand. You thought I was too stupid to figure out a way to read it. Like I don't know where to find a drugstore and wouldn't have a quarter in my purse."

"I didn't think it through."

"You didn't think, period. You're not stupid either. So why did you do it? Why insult me?"

They walked a quarter-block before he spoke.

"I was ashamed. I didn't have the imagination to spin something from whole cloth, so I exploited the woman I love. And I was afraid of losing her."

"You made up the pawnbroker. You told me that when you started writing the book. That was before you clammed up; which would be just about the time Marcy came in."

"He's based on every tough guy I saw in the movies. I'm a fraud.

I made such a fuss about research and not inventing anything, when the truth is I don't know how."

"Is this a trick? Confess to any piece of claptrap so I'll forgive you out of pity?"

"How's it working so far?"

She bumped against him hard. He had to scramble to keep his feet. "You're such a shit."

"It's the truth. I used to be able to cook from scratch: None of those things in my magazine stories ever happened. After I got home, they all seemed so phony I couldn't believe I'd ever thought I was a writer. Some guys came back missing arms and legs. I left my imagination back in Antwerp."

They waited at the corner for a street sweeper to gush past, then crossed. She was silent most of the way. Then she steered closer and took his arm. "It'll grow back."

———

They lay in her bed, spent and sweaty. A fan hummed on the sill of the open window, slinging cool air over them from outside as it swung their way. Ellen had a cigarette out, but just to play with.

"I didn't love him," she said.

"Who?" He'd begun to drift off.

"Him, idiot! Ann was wrong about that. She got the rest right."

He sat up. This was it: the Secret. "It must have been hard, though. She said he was killed."

"Who said he was killed?"

He stared; reached over and switched on the lamp on his side.

"Ann told you I lost him to the service," she said. "That's what you said before, and that's what she'd have said. It'd be a tidy little tragedy if he *was* killed, but I wouldn't wish it on him. I did enough to him as it was."

"What'd you do, break his heart?"

"Don't make it sound like I wrote him a Dear John letter. That's cheap."

"Sorry. Go ahead."

"His name was Harvey. We grew up in together. We were practically inseparable all through high school: You know, that couple that might as well be married, because that's how everyone thought of them. Me included. When he enlisted and proposed, I thought he already had. I said yes without giving it any thought. I mean, it was inevitable, right? But I was smart enough to postpone things until he came back. I didn't want to be a war widow. If this sounds callous—guilty as charged, officer.

"The marines sent him to the South Pacific. Over there he hooked up with a Filipino girl."

Jacob was silent. The story had taken a twist even a pulp writer couldn't foresee.

"I'm the one got the letter," she said. "Pathetic. He scourged himself all through it. 'I don't deserve forgiveness; you deserve better.' I was surprised the paper wasn't so tear-soaked it fell apart in my hands. And every line was a knife through my conscience. It was almost as bad as if we'd gone ahead with the wedding and lived the lie for the rest of our lives."

"Well—"

"Hold off on the comforting words. He was torn up with guilt. And I let him be."

She fumbled her lighter off her nightstand, lit the cigarette, blew smoke at the ceiling. "I never wrote him back. Of course he'd think I was angry and devastated. What else could he? I didn't want to tell him I never cared. I lied to myself that I was sparing his feelings. Telling him would've been more merciful."

"Where is he now?"

"Raising a herd of pearl-divers in Fiji. I get a card every Christmas, with a picture of the happy family."

"That's the big mystery?"

"Yup. What do you think?"

"Fuck him."

"What?"

"If he really believes he ruined your life, he must know he's twisting the knife every time he sends you a Kodak memory. So he's either a dope or a jerk. You dodged a bullet either way."

"I never thought of it like that."

"Neither did he. Imagine tying yourself to that blockhead till death you do part."

She took one last drag and stubbed out the butt. He hoped to cure her of smoking in bed.

"Now you know everything," she said. "Everything I plan to tell, anyway. Think you can get a book out of it?"

"I'm not sure. It depends on how long it takes my imagination to grow back."

She smacked his face, not really hard enough to sting.

They wrapped their limbs around each other and began the old ritual all over again. The fan reached them in gusts, chilling naked skin drenched in perspiration.

PART THREE

1950
ONE IN A MILLION

CHAPTER
TWENTY-FOUR

Scarpetti asked him what he thought of Truman.

"He's a hell of a haberdasher."

"Think he's going into Korea?"

"Nope. He'll send the army in his place."

"The son of a bitch."

Jacob changed the subject. The president was too far out of his reach. "Like your place?"

It was 1950. They were relaxing in the artist's new apartment on the Upper West Side. He'd taken it for the big front room with north light. The sound was off on the TV. A pair of middle-weights waltzed around a ring.

"I miss the loft. I liked the space and no neighbors. It's been months since I blew anything up." He sucked on the twisted brown cigarette between his thumb and forefinger, held the smoke, and let it stagger out, sinking like sediment into his arm-chair. Jacob sat facing him on the sofa. "I don't miss the stairs," Scarpetti said.

"How long have you been smoking reefers?"

"Since stir."

"How come I'm just finding out now?"

"I didn't know you so well before."

"It's been almost four years."

"I had to go easy. I won't get off as easy as Bob Mitchum."

"All this time, and you could have offered me a hit."

"Straight arrow like you?"

"Oh, I'm a Hollywood item now. They're flying me out next month."

"On the level?"

"I don't know about that, but Ira got a telegram from a producer named Kaspar. He wants *The Fence*, and me to write the screenplay."

"How many times has it gone back to print?"

"I lost count." The latest edition had a new cover by Scarpetti, with the anti-hero looking even more rakish and the heroine even more naked than the first time, plus a yellow banner: OVER 100,000 COPIES IN PRINT!

"This guy got the bucks?"

"Rolling in it. He has houses in Beverly Hills and Palm Springs, an apartment on Park Avenue, and an office in Rockefeller Center. He asked me which of those places I wanted to meet him, all expenses paid."

"No sense asking why you didn't say Rock Center." It was a gray drippy November.

"I might as well get some sun. It's all I'm likely to get."

"Bring me Rita Hayworth's autograph."

"I think she's in Africa or someplace with that potentate she married."

"Jane Russell, then. A signed photo."

"I'd've thought you'd be sick of tits."

Scarpetti looked at him quickly, then rolled his head back against the cushion. "It's different with their clothes on."

He passed the joint to Jacob, who set down his Scotch and drew the smoke in, coughing a little; he still wasn't a smoker, but his drinking skills were improving. "Where are you setting the next masterpiece?" His voice was squeezed.

"The waterfront. The air's too thin up here with the Vanderfellers."

"Sure. I was thinking Central Park, but you can make a ransom drop anywhere." Jacob paused. "It's a Fairfax."

"Christ. I hate that newshound."

Sylvester "Screamer" Fairfax—Jack Holly's invention—was a

crack reporter for the *New York Teller*, a tabloid based loosely on *The Greenwich Clock*. He was a one-man cop, judge, and jury, hounding gang bosses, white slavers, and corrupt politicians for front-page material.

"Elk likes him. The first one didn't do as well as *The Fence* or *Guns of Gotham*, but he thinks he'll build a following."

"He's always yelling, 'Stop the presses!' Did you ever once say that?"

"At the *Clock*? I never get the chance. Newsprint costs dough, and Sam Rosetti's cheap. Doesn't mean someone didn't say it somewhere, sometime."

"With Screamer it's all the time. When's he write his copy? You never sit him down at a typewriter."

"Would you pay two bits to watch him type?"

"Don't go by me. I get the books for free. Thanks for coming to my celebration, by the way."

"I didn't know this was a housewarming."

"It isn't. My parole ran out yesterday. I'm free to go to bars and associate with known felons."

"Haven't you been doing that right along?"

"Sure. But now it's legal."

"Where's the fun in that?"

———

Robin Elk announced *Down by the Docks*, the second "Screamer" Fairfax mystery, in the trades. The first printing sold out in a week. Jacob gave notice at *The Greenwich Clock*.

"You'll be back," Rosetti said. "TV's gonna kill books the way Detroit snuffed streetcars."

"They report the news on television, you know."

"The feds force 'em to. Madame Chiang can't compete with Milton Berle in a dress. Newspapers are here to stay."

He called Ellen to tell her he was now a full-time novelist. She met him at her door holding a bottle of bubbly and wearing nothing under a fur coat she'd borrowed from Phil Scarpetti's private prop department. That was the night she and Jacob became engaged.

———

"Welcome to L.A. How was your flight?"

Jacob thought. "High."

Edvard Kaspar chuckled. "Most say 'long.' Give me a writer with a sense of humor anytime. You can have Clifford Odets. He couldn't raise a giggle in a feather factory."

The producer was short and round, with a Polish accent and a tanned bald head, no hat. He wore a whipcord jacket, foulard scarf, chinos, and Italian loafers; only the beret and megaphone were missing. From the moment Kaspar met him at the bottom of the airplane steps, snatched his suitcase, and waddled ahead of him into the terminal, Jacob thought himself the victim of an elaborate practical joke.

Kaspar drove a wartime Cadillac with blackout headlights. The cracked leather upholstery smelled of garlic. He clipped red lights, braked inches from stopped cars, and changed lanes without signaling. By the time they got to his hotel, Jacob's jaws ached from clenching.

Phil Scarpetti would have described the hotel décor as Art Schizo. It was a cathedral of cream-colored stone, towering ludicrously over the horizontal architecture that surrounded it, like an upraised middle finger.

It was dusk. Just as they came to a tooth-chipping stop in front, a set of ground-mounted spotlights came on, bathing the façade in a pink glow.

"All for me?" Jacob peeled his foot from the firewall.

"You'll love it here. It's one of the city's oldest landmarks. Almost thirty years!"

He was spent from the long flight and the short ride. Kaspar said he'd pick him up in the morning and took off, tires chirping. Jacob carried his bag across a marble lobby the size of a train station, dotted with leather chairs and smoking stands. A petite female clerk found his reservation and the elevator took him to a room on the ninth floor, with a bathroom that sparkled and a swan-shaped bed on a dais. It was Garbo on a cracker.

———

"That's Harold Lloyd's house there on the right."

It was a sunny morning; Kaspar had stashed the smog behind the foothills for his guest.

Jacob stared out the window of the Cadillac, seeing only a wall of whitewashed brick.

"I thought Lloyd was dead."

"Retired. Saved his money, can you believe it? Mary Pickford too. Her place makes his look like a bungalow."

"*She's* still alive?"

"Nobody dies in Hollywood."

"What about Valentino?"

"He croaked in New York. This is where people go *after* they die."

Of course they dined at the Brown Derby. He saw no stars, ate corned beef hash while his host poked at watercress, drank fresh-squeezed orange juice, and held his tongue. Their waiter plugged a telephone into a jack and Kaspar made calls. There seemed to be a legal matter involved, but whether the producer was suing someone or being sued was unclear.

Today Kaspar wore a tweed jacket with elbow patches over a white silk shirt and another scarf, this one tied on one side of his thick neck pirate fashion. There was a crest of some kind on his cuff links.

He hung up the phone. "How'd you sleep?"

"So well I don't remember it."

"I knew you'd like the hotel. The linen's spun from Greer Garson's pubic hair."

Jacob choked on his orange juice.

"Ever write a screenplay?"

He mopped his shirtfront. "No, but I read the ones you sent. They're not that different from novels."

"You're one-up on most. I can't tell you how many writers I gave the boot because they thought they were writing theatrical plays for the screen: yak, yak, yak. We shot a Tarzan last year with just two sides of dialogue: Well, not counting the yell, and we dubbed that in from Weissmuller. Grossed two million on a budget of six hundred grand. Keep things moving, that's the secret."

"I saw it. The chimp got more screen time than Tarzan."

"That monkey was a sonofabitch. He bit Lex Barker on the cheek: eleven stitches. We had to shoot around him for two weeks, and you can't build a jungle picture on extras in black-face. We doped the monkey." He wiped his hands on his napkin. "Who do you see as Mike Cain?"

"Who?"

"The fence. Moynihan's too Irish. Cain's biblical. Can't go wrong with Holy Writ."

"That'd make him Jewish."

"Me too, but don't tell Breen in Standards and Practices; he's a fucking Nazi. Cain okay with you?"

"It's fine. Nobody remembers a character's name anyway, not counting Long John Silver and Zorro."

Kaspar grinned, showing bright veneers. "I knew we'd get on. Some of these pain-in-the-ass scribblers think they shit silver spoons." The accent gave his sailor's jargon an Old World flavor.

The formal tour began with the producer's offices in Century City, an open layout with only glass separating one workspace from another and a four-sheet poster of *Flesh and the Devil* on the wall above his desk. During the next three days Jacob watched Desi Arnaz beat a conga drum in the Trocadero, walked down New York Street on the studio's back lot, sat on Lana Turner's stool in Schwab's, and considered, suggested, and rejected Humphrey Bogart as Cain (too old), Virginia Mayo as Marcy

("Suspended," said Kaspar), and Dana Andrews as the police lieutenant ("Drying out in Sausalito").

In a souvenir shop on Sunset Boulevard he bought an autographed picture of Burt Lancaster, Ellen's favorite (they didn't have Jane Russell for Scarpetti), packed it in his carry-on, and rode back to LAX with Kaspar. The producer talked all the way through the congealing traffic.

"Put in lots of pussy. Breen don't like it, but you can bootleg it. We can't take the girl's clothes off like on your covers, but you'd be surprised what you can do with an exposed bra strap. Pussy, that's what sells tickets."

Jacob shook hands and climbed the steps to his plane. At the top he turned around for one last wave. Kaspar cupped his hands around his mouth and shouted, "Pussy!"

The writer smiled wanly at a disapproving stewardess.

"College nickname," he said.

———

Back home, he called Ira Winderspear.

"Kaspar's a clown," he told the agent, "but they grow them there like oranges. I think he liked me. If the money's right, I'm writing the screenplay."

"Not so fast, kid. I just got off the phone with him. He's hired a local, pro with a box-office record. My guess? He brought you out there to Jew the guy down on his price."

"Oh." He didn't know whether he was disappointed or just worn out. "Well, I got to see Harold Lloyd's wall."

"Hold your horses, I'm not finished. Kaspar wants to option the book for ten grand: another twenty thousand guaranteed on beginning of principal photography, whatever the hell that is. Could be just Californian for the old shafteroo; but like they say in the horse operas, I gotcha covered. Congratulations, kid. You're in show business."

CHAPTER
TWENTY-FIVE

"So how was Tinseltown, apart from screwing you over?" Ellen asked.

"It's just like you see in movies."

"Explain."

"Movie New York isn't New York. It *looks* like New York, sort of, but the soot's sprayed on and the horns don't honk right. But Hollywood's Hollywood. They take it down and stick it back up between productions."

"What else?"

"Kaspar says Van Johnson's a fairy."

"Who doesn't know that? He's prettier than I am."

"*You* said it. *I* didn't."

They were in bed in his apartment. The television was on in the living room, loud enough for Ellen to follow *Your Hit Parade*, her favorite program. Snooky Lanson, the host, was trying to sing rhythm-and-blues. She traced the spiral in Jacob's ear with a finger. "Crestfallen?"

"Where'd you get that word? You've been cheating on me with Dostoevsky."

"I only read this guy Holly. Someday he's going to write a masterpiece. They'll bind it in leather and give him the Pulitzer Prize. They'll make him a professor at Columbia—the university, not the movie studio—and he'll go to work every day wearing a corduroy coat with patches on the elbows."

"That's how Kaspar dresses, when he's not in riding breeches. He can't make up his mind whether he's Erich von Stroheim or Arthur Miller."

"Is Desi Arnaz as handsome in person as he looks in *Billboard*?"

"Now you're cheating on me with a bongo player."

"Listen to you. For all I know you went out dancing every night with Yvonne De Carlo."

"Like you wouldn't dance with Burt Lancaster."

They tired of the game. She reached across him, brushing his bare chest with a breast, and retrieved a cigarette and a book of matches from the nightstand.

"I wish you'd give those up," he said. "This place is starting to smell like a back room in Tammany Hall."

"I'll make you a deal." She shook out the match and blew smoke toward the other side of the bed. "I'll quit smoking when you cut back on your drinking. You were practically teetotal when we met. Now you're never out of reach of a glass."

"I don't even keep liquor here."

"You don't need it, with three bars on your street and a setup waiting every time you drop in on Phil Scarpetti."

"I guess maybe I've been identifying too much with the people I write about." He smiled. "Okay. From now on I stop at one snort."

"In that case—" She leaned across him again, pressing harder against his chest, and ground the cigarette out in the copper ashtray. Before she could retreat to her side of the bed, he grabbed her and kissed her deep.

Later, she sat up and planted her chin on his shoulder. "What do you think of June?"

"Rhymes with 'spoon,' 'moon,' and 'pontoon.' I sure know how to stink as a poet."

"You know we're discussing a date for the wedding."

"Why June? I spend most of my time trying to avoid clichés. I suppose you want to go to Niagara Falls afterwards."

"Maybe. I can be corny even if you can't."

"Didn't you ever wonder why a bridegroom would consider going to a place with a hundred-and-sixty-foot drop onto solid rocks?"

She pulled back. "Are you having reservations?"

"Yeah, if they're with a hotel in Niagara Falls. I'd be up ten times a night going to the bathroom."

"Okay, we'll table the honeymoon. Let's talk about the service. Do you want a rabbi?"

"My Hebrew's rusty."

"Any kind of church wedding?"

"You mean veils and a top hat? Okay, if it's a deal-breaker."

"As romantic as you make it sound, I don't see myself shoving a cake in your face. There's always city hall."

"Why not Blue Devil? We can get a preacher, and Elk's secretary Alice can take pictures."

"Swell. I'll make one of Hank Stratton's hookers my maid of honor. Let's start over. You suggest a date."

"February twenty-ninth."

"There isn't one this year. You want to wait two years?"

"Look at it from my perspective. I wouldn't have to buy you an anniversary gift until 1956."

"You're impossible. And I'm going home." She slid out of bed and hooked on her bra.

He put his hands behind his head and watched. "Free for lunch tomorrow?"

She paused with one leg inside her slip. "What makes you think—"

"*Shh!*" He pushed himself into a sitting position.

"Are you telling me to shut up?"

He waggled a hand, tilting his head toward the living room, where the TV was still playing.

". . . the pervasive and toxic influence of the publishers who deal in this filth."

Your Hit Parade had ended and the news was on. The shrill female voice came through louder than the musical numbers.

He tore aside the covers, got up, and bounded naked past Ellen into the living room, lit only by the blue glow of the picture tube.

The woman who'd spoken, whoever she was, had stopped. John Cameron Swayze's earnest face filled the screen.

"That was Margery St. John, the Democratic congresswoman from Nebraska, who today pressed for the appointment of a congressional committee to investigate charges of subversion and pornography in the publishing industry. She announced plans to subpoena testimony from parents, teachers, clergymen, police officers, publishers, and writers, and call upon industry representatives to show cause why they should not be indicted for acts of sedition and contributing to the delinquency of thousands of minors.

"Mrs. St. John expressed particular concern over one branch of publishing: The manufacturers and distributors of paperback novels."

The newsman put aside a sheet of paper and smiled. "We pause now for a few words from Timex."

CHAPTER
TWENTY-SIX

Robin Elk hung up the phone and looked across his desk at his visitors. "That was Fritz Waterman, my attorney. He's not a Constitutional scholar, but he thinks we're shielded by the First Amendment; a distinct improvement, I must say, over our Official Secrets Act back home."

"That's what Henry Miller's lawyer said." Phil Scarpetti put out a cigarette in the stand next to his chair. "It didn't stop the Coast Guard from dumping an entire shipment of *Tropic of Capricorn* into the harbor last year. We've come a long way since the Boston Tea Party."

"Forgive me, Phil, but why are you here? Mrs. St. John made no mention of artists in her address."

"Moral support," said Jacob.

Scarpetti shook his head. "Sorry, Jake, but I learned in the can not to stick my neck out for anybody but yours truly. It's just a matter of time before she gets around to me. It's the covers that got her attention. Politicians only read summaries written by aides. Why wade halfway through *Down by the Docks* to get to the brothel scene when it's right up front?"

Jacob winced. "That scene ran a page and a half, and the nudity was only implied."

"You can't imply in oils. I'm the one who found the bondage theme in *Jane Eyre*, don't forget."

"In retrospect, I regret approving that design," said Elk. "The Brontës were my favorite when I was at school."

"When was the last time any of them sold forty thousand copies?"

"How serious is this threat?" Jacob said. "How many of these freshman representatives have any real power?"

"I'm not sure if 'fresh*man*' is the proper term in this case; but we're not here to discuss gender." The publisher looked at the pad he'd scribbled on during the phone consultation. "Fritz did his homework. She's thirty-six, a widowed mother of two children in elementary school. Her public service is rather in the way of an inheritance. The Honorable Conrad St. John was running for re-election when he suffered a fatal stroke. She took up the reins; and as it seems to be a challenge for voters in the Corn Belt to embrace a new player from out of nowhere, the good people of Nebraska cast their ballots for the surname."

Jacob said, "I grew up in the Midwest. We vote like everyone else, hoping the next one isn't worse than the last. What I want to know is can she do what she says?"

"As you indicated, few in Congress make much of an impression during their first term. What bills they manage to introduce perish in committee. However, if they stumble upon an issue that resonates beyond their own constituency—well, I'm sure you're aware of what's been happening in the motion picture industry."

"That's about Communism." Scarpetti lit another cigarette. "I'm not a Red. Jake's a Republican, so he's in the clear. What about you, Elk? You a Robin red-breast?"

"Who said I was a Republican?" Jacob put in.

"You don't like Truman."

"Who does, including Bess?"

Elk broke in. "In answer to your question, no, I'm not a Communist. I doubt Mrs. St. John would know Joe Stalin from Joe McCarthy, nor care. As a PTA mother she's more concerned with the corruption of our nation's youth through the glamorization of sex and violence. She threw in sedition merely to draw support from across the aisle."

"Sex is pretty damn glamorous without our help," Scarpetti said. "As for violence, Jake blew up his guy in *The Fence* and plopped his severed arm smack dab in the middle of Columbus

Circle. If we're doing anything, we're turning kids *against* violence by showing it for what it is; not like in movies, where they spray bullets like Flit and guys grab their chests and fall over without bleeding."

"There's been grumbling about that as well, at least where television is concerned. The crusaders keep count of the corpses that spill into the nation's living rooms every evening; but that may be to our benefit, if it draws the fire away from us. And let's not overlook the collateral effect. When *TV Guide* called *Lash Logan, Private Eye* 'a sadistic feast,' sales of Hank Stratton's books doubled. He doesn't even have anything to do with the series creatively." Elk sat back, twirling the crook of his cane.

"That doesn't let me off the hook," said Jacob. "This could kill the Hollywood deal."

"No need for concern. You have a contract, and Blue Devil has agreed to issue a new edition of *The Fence* with the star's likeness on the cover, whomever he turns out to be. The book will sell tickets and the movie will sell books. Our rustic congresswoman would have to have a great deal in her bag of tricks to overcome that. Gentlemen, this is a feather in the breeze. At all events, Blue Devil is in your corner. We share the same risks."

Scarpetti's grin was bitter. "*The U.S. v. Blue Devil Books.* I want to paint the cover."

The Goliath Typewriter Mart had more machines on display than he'd ever seen in one place, including the offices of the *Clock*: They lined shelves in every make and model, some tagged for repair, others on sale new and used, and the odor of ink, oil, and solvent was a physical presence. The new International Business Machines electric had its own pedestal, with a printed card listing its price and features. It was mostly motor and as big as a mangle.

A dusty window in the partition in back looked into a mechanical charnel-house: naked chassis, sprung springs, broken cogs, and spools of tattered ribbon spread out like entrails. A graybeard in a smeared apron bent over a bench, dismantling a McKinley-era Oliver with a screwdriver.

The counterman, ten years younger than Jacob and wearing a white lab coat, frowned at Jacob's Remington, lifted the occasional key with the eraser end of an unsharpened pencil, pressed a thumbnail into the rubber sheathing the platen, and let out a whistle.

"How long have you had this machine?"

"Four years."

"You sure gave it a workout. These portables aren't designed for heavy use."

The finish was as glossy as ever, but he'd worn most of the lettering off the keys. Lately his copy had begun to look like a ransom note, letters wandering above and below the line and some barely leaving an impression. The machine worked as hard and as reliably as always, but the results weren't the same. Seabiscuit was turning into a milk horse.

"It hasn't failed me in two hundred thousand words."

"What are you, a stenographer?"

"Worse. Writer."

"Would I know your stuff?"

"I doubt it."

"E. B. White came in just last month. *Stuart Little*? Turned out all he needed was a good cleaning."

"Can you fix the strikers?"

The bright eagerness went out of the clerk's face. Jacob thought maybe he should have asked him something about E. B. White. "You need a new platen."

"I asked about the strikers."

"The platen's what threw them out of line. The rubber gets hard and loses its flexibility. We can realign the strikers, but without a new platen, they'll be back out of line again in no time."

"How much for the realignment?"

"They need to be pried loose and resoldered; that's a time-eater. Cost you forty. Platen'll run another ten."

"I could get a new typewriter for that." He seemed to have had this conversation before.

"I would. Something else is bound to break, probably the space-bar mechanism, which is a pain to replace. That IBM's a steal at three hundred, and it'll still be going after ten of these relics have gone to scrap."

"I don't know anything about electrics."

"They're the future."

"The present's fine with me. I don't write science fiction."

"Let's give it a try."

One of the hard-sell boys; there was a commission in it for him. Jacob wanted to walk out, but he'd been to three places already and the prognosis hadn't changed.

The mechanism seemed simple enough, but the young man insisted on coming around the counter anyway. He cranked in two sheets and flipped a switch. The motor made a whirring noise like a tank engine. "Needs to warm up."

"My Remington doesn't."

"Go ahead, take it for a test drive."

He frowned at the square keys, touched a key. The machine chattered, typing *jjjjjjjjj* across the page. He jerked back his hand as if a snake had struck at it.

"I don't need that many *j*'s to write my name."

"You're not letting the machine do the work. All you have to do is touch it. Here." He tapped a different key; the carriage swooshed all the way to the right and stopped with a clunk at the left margin, one line down. He flicked a key. Jacob looked at the sheet.

"That's a *j*, all right. Can I see a manual?"

"You're making a mistake."

"At least I'm making them one at a time."

He left with a slightly used Smith-Corona standard on sale for twenty-five dollars; the clerk allowed him five bucks in trade on the Remington for replacement parts. It took a different ribbon, so he bought a spare for six bits. He felt sick leaving behind the machine that had jump-started his life. It was as if he'd brought a faithful old dog to the vet for a worming, then put him down instead.

And he couldn't shake the uneasy sensation that his luck was about to change for the worse.

CHAPTER
TWENTY-SEVEN

They set the date: June, in a small ballroom in a downtown hotel that was booked through October, but had a miraculous last-minute cancellation. Phil Scarpetti had placed a brief call to Ellen, advising her to try the hotel again. He didn't identify the source of his information.

"Spill," Jacob said, when they were smoking an illegal substance in the artist's apartment. "It was one of your shady contacts, wasn't it?"

"Nothing so sinister. I'm Carmelita's son Philip, not Pittsburgh Phil. The bride got caught shoplifting in the store where she was registered. Groom-to-be bugged out."

"How'd you manage that?"

"I didn't plant the stuff on her, if that's what you mean. I've got friends in store security all over town."

"I'm relieved. I considered asking Irish Mickey Shannon for a favor, but since I never heard from him after *The Fence* came out I didn't want to press my luck."

Scarpetti blew smoke out his nostrils. "You still might, when he gets out. The state gave him time to catch up on his reading."

"Prison?"

"Short stretch, and he was lucky to get it. He sold a set of steak knives to a detective from the Third Precinct. It had the governor's crest on the box."

"He must not have read my book." Jacob felt woozy. He snuffed out his butt and laid it in the ashtray. "Where are you taking me for my bachelor party?"

"That's a surprise."

"Tell me you're not planning to throw a bag over my head and kidnap me to some roadhouse. I'll go into cardiac arrest. Any minute now, Frank Costello might recognize himself as Blinky Fantonetti, the Juke King of Jersey."

"Simmer down. Nobody recognizes himself in books. Where's the ceremony?"

"United Church of Christ on Houston, the Reverend Charles Odell presiding. I met him at the *Clock*. He likes Chinese."

"Ellen okayed him?"

"She'd be okay with the captain of the Staten Island ferry." He paused. "Phil?"

"Um-hum?"

"I couldn't think of anyone else I'd want to stand up for me."

"I couldn't think of anyone else who'd trust me not to hock the ring."

Scarpetti took a suite in the wedding hotel for the stag party. Robin Elk attended, along with Skip Glaser, his art director, and Howard Belknap, the Blue Devil receptionist in the horn-rimmed glasses. Several brands and varieties of whiskey occupied a low table and cigar smoke hazed the air. Young Belknap declined a cigar, but after a few sips of bourbon he tried one, and spent the next ten minutes in the bathroom.

Someone knocked. Scarpetti ushered in a diminutive blonde dressed like Annie Oakley, all in white, from her cowboy hat to her high-heeled boots. Rhinestones crusted her short fringed skirt and suede vest, which covered only her nipples. She carried a portable phonograph.

"Which one's the bridegroom?" She beamed.

He pointed his cigar. "The one with his tongue hanging out."

She set down the record player and switched her hips Jacob's way. She threw her arms around him and grinned up. Her perfume stung his eyes. "My name's Calamity. What's yours?"

"Jack." He said it without thinking.

"Sit down, Jack." She splayed a palm against his chest and shoved. He fell into an armchair.

Her record collection was all western. By the time Bing Crosby and the Andrews Sisters finished "I'm an Old Cowhand (from the Rio Grande)," she was down to her hat, boots, and a pair of red panties embroidered with a gold lariat. Howard, recovered from his cigar emergency, flushed furiously when she shook her breasts in his face. They were clad only in pasties shaped like tiny sheriff's stars. Elk, equally red-faced, but from drink (Jacob had never seen him imbibe more than a glass of wine at lunch), shook his head smiling as she approached him, so she turned to Glaser. The gaunt man showed no reaction as she straddled his lap, grinding her crotch against his; for the hundredth time, Jacob wondered who had nicknamed him Skip.

Jacob got the same treatment, but only briefly. He took firm hold of her shoulders and gave her a gentle push. Without losing her smile, she kissed him on the lips and got up, dancing toward Scarpetti, sitting on the sofa.

He grinned, cigar clamped between his teeth, as she ground herself against him. She started to unzip his fly.

He shot upright, spilling her to the floor. She landed on her tailbone.

"Hey!"

Stooping, he grasped her arm and jerked her to her feet. He dug a roll of cash from a pocket and peeled off several bills. "Show's over, Calamity. The stage is pulling out." He stuffed the money into her panties.

"Son of a bitch motherfucker." She dressed quickly and swept out carrying her phonograph.

Scarpetti addressed the silence in the room.

"When I take out my dick it's my idea." He twisted out his cigar in an ashtray. "And I don't pay for it."

Elk was the first to react, with a characteristically abashed laugh. "It's better than my family motto. I wonder if it would translate into Latin."

The drinking resumed. Belknap passed out in his chair. Scarpetti went into the bedroom, brought back a blanket, and spread it over him. Elk, on his third Irish whisky, kept the conversation going.

"My first ambition was to be a ballroom dancer," he said. "I saw *Top Hat* at an impressionable age when it showed in London. The pater threw a fit, but I was determined. I have Jerry to thank for sparing me the worst." He tapped one of his slippered feet with his cane. "Did you always want to write?" he asked Jacob.

"No. I guess I can thank that foreman in the Battery for how I turned out."

The publisher changed the subject; despite his choice of literary subject matter, his POW experience seemed to have left him with a low tolerance for violent interaction. "And you, Skip? Born with the itch to draw?"

The art director was sketching in a hotel pad. "I was going to be Bud Fisher."

"Who's that? Baseball player, I suppose. All you red-blooded Yanks want your picture on a bubble-gum card."

"He's a cartoonist, Lord Fauntleroy. *Mutt and Jeff*?"

Elk, blowing smoke rings, shook his head.

Glaser turned the pad around. He'd drawn a facsimile of the tall gaunt drifter of comics in the straw boater and his short, silk-hatted companion. "My father died when I was six. My mother got a job in a pulp mill. She was always bringing home reams of paper for me to scribble on."

"What happened?" Jacob said.

"I came to a bad end." He tore off the sheet, crumpled it, and slammed it into the wastebasket.

"Phil?" Elk said. "Who did you want to be?"

"Machine Gun Kelly."

"Surely *that's* a baseball name."

"He was a thug," Glaser said. "Don't you read anything besides *Punch*?" He was palpably drunk.

"Well. It seems no one in this room quite turned out as planned."

"All except Calamity," said Jacob.

Even Scarpetti laughed.

━━━━━

The ceremony, in the hotel ballroom, was brief and informal; the guests applauded when the couple kissed. The Reverend Odell shook Jacob's hand, kissed Ellen—radiant in a powder-blue suit and matching pillbox hat with a brief veil—accepted the envelope from the bridegroom with a discreet gesture, and left for a funeral in Westchester.

The reception followed in the same room. Robin Elk was first in the receiving line—peck on the cheek and an unaffected glistening in his eyes—then Scarpetti, followed by a critic from *The Post* who'd stuck out his neck to review *Down by the Docks* favorably ("and got mail, I can tell you, from the archdiocese"), Ellen's old roommate Ann (six months' pregnant with her husband, a dull-but-successful plumbing contractor in Queens), the entire Blue Devil staff, and sundry acquaintances of whose connection to the occasion Jacob was only dimly aware.

Cliff Cutter was the only writing colleague invited. There was a dignity about the old westerner that could only add to the occasion. He brought along his wife, a small round American Indian whose moon face might have been fashioned from terra-cotta. She presented Ellen with a small stone carving of an animal attached to a braided leather thong, to be worn around the neck. "Wear tonight," she said. "In nine months, a child."

Jacob snatched it as Ellen was opening her purse. He stuck it in his pocket. "It goes into a safe-deposit box."

A jazz combo Scarpetti had found in a neighborhood club took the bandstand. Between sets, Ellen mounted the platform and threw the bouquet over her shoulder. Alice, Elk's secretary, caught it. Howard Belknap blushed.

"You know the truth about marriage, right?" Scarpetti, buttonholing the groom, breathed pure gin from the open bar into his face, a heavy hand on his shoulder.

"I've heard theories. I'm sure you can add to them."

"It's like belonging to the Pinup-of-the-Month Club; only it's the same girl, month in and month out, for the rest of your life."

"You're sloshed, Scarpetti."

"That's the effect I was going for."

Ellen's mother came up. She was a shorter, broader version of her daughter, but a handsome woman of fifty, in a brocaded jacket over a ruffled blouse and floor-length skirt, with a corsage the size of a cauliflower pinned to one lapel. She smiled at Scarpetti. "Well, hello, there, do you remember me?"

For once the artist was stuck for a reply.

"Don't you remember? You liked my spaghetti."

He spluttered. "I didn't know you without your hairnet! But you must've served meals to—"

"Thousands. But only one with a compliment."

"That's because your sauce didn't come from a can."

"I did my own shopping. Are you behaving yourself?"

"It's a struggle. I've searched five boroughs looking for your recipe."

"The secret's brown sugar; but don't tell anyone. I'm opening a restaurant after I retire."

"I'm no stoolie." He stooped to buss her on the cheek.

After he excused himself, Jacob approached her. "I wondered if you knew each other."

"I was glad when he was released," she said. "Prison's dangerous for men like him."

"Artists?"

She smiled at him. "I'm so happy he was your best man. You're a true friend."

───

They honeymooned in the Catskills; a compromise. Jacob said, "How many kids do you want? I'm thinking ten, in case nine of them turn out no good."

"I thought you didn't want children right away."

"That was just for public consumption. I'm all ready to start the next generation of juvenile delinquent."

"In that case, I better put this on." She took the wedding gift from Cliff Cutter's wife out of her purse.

"How'd you get that?"

"Picked your pocket while you were in the shower."

He looked at the carving. "I think it's some kind of weasel. I hope the kids are better looking."

She gave him a humid kiss. "Let's start with Jacob Heppleman, Junior, and see how he turns out."

"Jack."

"I thought you hated that."

"I'm warming to it. It's brought me luck."

"Let's start with conception and do the rest later."

"Okay, but I need to practice."

And they did. Three months later, Ellen came back from her doctor's office wearing a huge smile.

"Damn," said her husband. "Someone should call the cops. That weasel's a concealed weapon."

CHAPTER
TWENTY-EIGHT

Robin Elk's voice was jovial; but then it usually was, whatever the news. "I wanted to be the first to congratulate you."

"How'd you find out? We haven't told anyone yet."

"I might ask the same thing. I just got the word."

"Did Ellen tell you?"

"She knows, too?"

"Let's start over," Jacob said. "What's your news?"

"Edvard Kaspar called to tell me which movie star to put on the cover of the new edition of *The Fence*. It seems you're now in the picture business. He's sending a crew to shoot background footage next week: The *B* unit, it's called. You'd think they'd have all New York on film by now; but Hollywood never misses the chance to spend money."

"I'll be damned."

"What's *your* news?" Elk said.

He told him about the baby.

Elk chuckled. "Well, then, double the congratulations, and please extend them to your lovely bride. When is the happy event?"

"The doctor says March. Who'd Kaspar get to play Moynihan?"

"Cain, you mean. Some fellow named Victor Mature; an invented appellation, no doubt. Do you know him? I'm woefully ignorant on the subject of U.S. cinema stars; apart from Fred Astaire, of course."

"He's better than I'd hoped, but he plays heroes. Now I suppose he's receiving and selling stolen merchandise to pay for his mother's operation."

"Are you upset?"

"No. You can't ruin something that's already finished. Have you told Phil? He'll want to get photos and scrounge up a model who bears some resemblance."

"I have: There's a time factor, otherwise I'd have notified you first as a matter of courtesy. Shall I quote his reaction, or would you prefer I paraphrase?"

"I'm not a child, Robin."

"Very well." He cleared his throat, and delivered a fair impression of Scarpetti's Brooklyn accent. "'You mean the liver-lipped weightlifter who played Doc Holliday in *My Darling Clementine?*' I'm at a loss as to the reference."

"Will Scarpetti do it?"

"Of course he will. He's a professional."

The launch party for the new edition of *The Fence* was more subdued than the first celebration Jacob had attended at Blue Devil. The music came from a cabinet phonograph in Elk's office, and the gathering was smaller. Cliff Cutter sent his regrets from his camp in New Mexico, where he was researching a new western, and Hugh Brock—whose *Invisible Aliens* had been picked up by a suddenly science-fiction-hungry Hollywood—was in New York General, undergoing psychiatric treatment after a little-known incident at the Bronx Zoo ("Even the tabloids can't find a way to report a romantic encounter with a zebra that will pass inspection," said Phil Scarpetti), and Hank Stratton was in California, serving as a technical advisor for *Lash Logan's* second season on CBS; the *TV Guide* pan had paid off in ratings.

Phoebe Sternwalter—P. B. Collier—asked Ellen's permission to touch her swelling abdomen, and predicted a son. She sighed. "Another aggressive member of the male population to make war on our gender." She shook a finger in Jacob's face. "Don't give him a toy gun."

Jacob, grinning with fatherly pride—and the effects of an open bar—said, "I can't give him a *real* one, Phoebe. Dr. Spock wouldn't approve."

Burt Woods and Paul Arthur came up to them separately, as was their habit. "Just don't let them cast William Demarest as the detective," Woods said. "He turned our Inspector Spang into a buffoon."

Arthur: "Don't listen to Burt. He wanted Ed Wynn."

Robin Elk tapped his glass to command attention. Hooking his cane over one arm, he snatched the sheet off an easel, showing Victor Mature at the pawnshop counter with a familiar-looking blonde stripping in the background.

"Grace Kelly?" said Jacob. "Has she been cast?"

Elk shook his head. "Kaspar wants her on the cover anyway. I ran it past Lawyer Waterman. He says celebrities are public figures, and less entitled than the rest of us to sue for invasion of privacy."

Ellen said, "Why not Bess Truman?"

"She wouldn't return my calls." Scarpetti was drunk as usual.

Elk said, "We're running a banner: OVER ONE MILLION COPIES IN PRINT."

"I'm one in a million." Jacob put his arm around Ellen's waist. "What do you think?"

She patted her stomach. "I think Jack, Junior must never be told where you got Marcy."

As the gathering dispersed, Elk pulled Jacob aside.

"Splendid news. Mrs. St. John—I should say the Honorable Margery St. John of the great state of Nebraska—is a dead issue. Her request for a hearing on the industry has been denied."

"Who killed it?"

"The Speaker of the House. He's retiring at the end of his term to write his memoirs. Someone explained to him the benefits of issuing them in a format his constituents can afford."

"I almost feel sorry for her."

"One roots for the underdog. It's the American way, yes? Yes." Elk twirled his cane and propelled himself toward the bar, manned by Howard Belknap.

"Victor Mature?" Jacob said to Scarpetti.

The artist shrugged. "I was just happy I could fit his shoulders on the canvas."

Jacob glanced across Elk's office at Ellen, who was admiring the tiny diamond on Alice's left hand; she and Belknap were engaged.

"If you'd told me four years ago I'd love this old barn, I'd've laughed in your face."

"You're sloshed, Heppleman."

It looked like a scene in one of his books: *White Gold*, about the white slavery racket in Chinatown. A man in a slouch hat and trench coat was reading a newspaper under the corner streetlamp half a block from their apartment.

Jacob didn't think anything of it at first. The man didn't look up as he passed. There was a light rain falling, and there was no law against dressing like Hank Stratton; but why pause in the rain to read a newspaper?

It was only when he was climbing the stairs to the apartment that it sank in: The paper was in Hebrew.

Ellen was staying overnight in Ossining, where her mother was hosting a baby shower attended by some of Ellen's friends from work.

He had his key out when the door opened away from it.

His heart jumped. He looked straight ahead, then down at a stunted figure standing inside his home. Irish Mickey Shannon looked even smaller now. He'd lost weight behind bars, shrinking his face and redefining the bones. With chin unshaven and a cloth cap pulled low over his bulging eyes, he looked like a police artist's sketch based on an eyewitness description; the features were that exaggerated.

The effect was increased by a scruffy brown leather jacket worn over a heavy orange turtleneck. Tan slacks covered his stumpy legs and his feet were shoved into sneakers plainly bought in the boys' department.

He made a motion with an ugly blue Luger. It was a swollen thing in his hand, a cartoon blunderbuss. It should have been comical; it wasn't. He stuck it under his belt.

"Sorry about the artillery, Jackie boy. You never know who you might run into this late."

"How'd you get in?" He heard his voice quaver.

"You pick things up in the joint. You need a better lock and an unlisted number. Ain't it past your bedtime?"

"I was visiting a friend."

Shannon sniffed, looking like a Pekingese. "Mary Jane's my guess. That's illegal. Take a load off."

He thought of trying for the stairs. Then he remembered the man under the streetlamp. He stepped inside. The dwarf kicked the door shut.

"Nice dump. Kid on the way, you'll need more room."

Jack and Ellen stood smiling in a framed photo on a table, she with a hand on her swelling stomach. She was five months along.

"What's the idea, Mickey?"

"Take a load off, I said."

He sat, in the rocker they'd bought to put the baby to sleep. Shannon took a seat in Jacob's overstuffed chair; squirmed around, jerked the pistol from his belt, and laid it on an end table. He took the new edition of *The Fence* from inside his jacket.

"Found it in J. C. Penney's. What I wonder is why I had to spend two bits when you was to show it to me before it got in print."

"I sent you the galleys."

"Galleys, what's that?"

"Early proofs. You're a busy guy. Maybe you forgot all about 'em."

Shannon stared at him without blinking.

"Could be. I ain't much of a reader. Also when I made bail after the pinch I had to find a billet where the cops couldn't tail me to my warehouse." He looked at the back cover. "'Soon to be a Major Motion Picture.' You must be rolling in it."

"I haven't seen a penny yet."

He didn't seem to be listening. "I guess you heard about my trouble."

"Anybody can make a mistake."

"Somebody tipped off that cop."

"Mickey, it wasn't me."

"Scraps, maybe."

"Not Phil either. What would be the point? We both got what we wanted."

"Don't get your panties in a wad. I thought it was one of you, you'd both be dead. But I can't go near my stuff till the heat's off, and I'm tapped. I need a loan."

"I thought all you guys knew somebody."

"The sharks expect to be paid back. Way I see it, since I was your whatchacall inspiration, you might return the favor."

"You think Mike Moynihan is you, don't you?" Jacob shook his head. "I talked to a lot of people, did a lot of reading. In the end I made him up. That's why it's called fiction. Look at the cover. He look anything like you?"

"Cut the bullshit, Jack. Dames buy books. I'd still have my cherry if I didn't know how to raise dough. Personally, I think this bird looks like a wop gigolo, but there's no accounting for taste."

He tapped the book. "I open this up to any page, I hear me talking. Everything I told you's in here. My name should be on the cover right next to yours."

Jacob relaxed a little. This was Isidore Muntz, the midget jockey from Tijuana, not Baby Face Nelson. "How much, Mickey? Five hundred? A thousand?"

"I wouldn't sting you for a grand; not all in a lump. You're a fambly man, got to worry about diapers and college. We'll go on the easy payment plan. Five hundred down, a yard a month. When the movie comes out we'll renegotiate."

Jacob had had enough. The little man had seen too many movies in stir. "No dice, Mickey. Where would it end? Get the hell out of my house. You're on parole. Just having that pistol can put you back inside."

Mickey's face congested; turned almost black. His breath wheezed through his squashed nose. "I told you things I almost got kilt to learn! It was my gift to you and you sold it to every bum on the street for two bits!"

He paused, looked embarrassed; shook himself and smiled, showing stumpy yellow teeth with black gums. "Take a hinge out that window."

"Why, you going to throw me out it, shrimp like you?"

"I could shoot you in the back." He took the pistol, kicked out the magazine, put it in his pocket, and ejected the cartridge from the chamber. Nodded toward the window.

Jacob stood and looked out. The man on the corner had put away his newspaper. He was staring up at the window.

Jacob laughed almost hysterically. It was the old Jew from Mickey's brownstone. He was absurd in street clothes.

Then, seeing Jacob, he reached inside the right sleeve of his trench coat and withdrew something that glinted under the streetlamp: An ice pick ground down to a razor point.

"Sid used to collect for Dutch Schultz," Mickey said. "He's got rheumatism now, and it makes him testy. It ain't so bad he can't stick you in the heart someday in a crowd.

"You know what the witnesses always say," he added: "'Officer, it all happened so fast.'"

Jacob went into the bedroom, unwrapped his .45 from a towel on the top shelf of the linen closet, checked the load, in case Mickey had found it and disarmed it, and went back into the living room. Shannon stood with his hands in his pockets, the Luger in his belt.

"Scram, you little squirt. Take the Golem with you."

"You don't want to do this, Jack. Think about Mrs. Hepple-man, and little Jake, Junior, if you're lucky and it's a boy. Don't he want to be born?"

"If I see you and your goon anywhere near me or my family, I'll put you both down like dogs."

"It ain't like in your books. The holes don't bleed clean and help don't come in the nick of time. It's the innocent bystanders get the shaft." He went to the door. "My turf next time." He opened it and went out.

CHAPTER
TWENTY-NINE

"Give me a ring when it's settled." Ira Winderspear hung up and passed a hand over his bald brown head. Clouds hung below his window in the Chrysler Building, but they didn't make him look any more like Zeus on Mount Olympus.

He smiled at Jacob. "Reason you haven't seen a penny of that twenty g's is the production shut down after shooting the street stuff. It doesn't kick in till one of the actors shows up in costume and makeup. That's what 'principal photography' means according to Edvard Kaspar."

"How'd you reach him? I can't get past his secretary."

"I sent her chocolates for her birthday. Keep a calendar, kid, that's my advice."

"What did that cost me?"

"Not a cent. My brother-in-law has a confectionery in Jersey. I get 'em by the case."

"They said they'd wrap by spring. It's spring, and you're telling me they haven't even started yet?"

"You're not alone in the boat. Kaspar says the whole industry's shut down till they settle a union argument. It all has to do with Eve Arden's tits."

"Come again?"

"The actress? She was shooting a scene at RKO when the director said cut: She's too flat-chested, it's a distraction. Do I need to add he dated Jane Russell?"

"I think you just did."

"So he called Wardrobe and ordered a pair of falsies. Well,

somebody in the makeup department got wind of it and said falsies aren't Wardrobe, they're Makeup. So the director switched the order. Then Wardrobe complained to the union: Sewing a pair of Brillo pads in a brassiere is Wardrobe. The Makeup union filed a counter-complaint, and that's where it's stood for weeks. Everything's stalled till the parties get together and work it out."

"A strike?"

"Same as. *Variety* wanted to run a headline: 'Eve's Apples,' but the Breen Office threatened to pull all the studio advertising, so they killed it. Meanwhile nothing's getting done."

"Jesus, Ira. I just put down six thousand on a house on Long Island. Ellen's due next week. I'm going to bounce checks all over town because Eve Arden's breasts don't?"

"Don't panic. The Academy's appointed a mediator, and both sides agree to abide with his decision. How much you need to tide you over? The new edition of *The Fence* starts paying royalties next month. You won't owe me long."

"I hate to be a mooch. I was better off broke."

"It's expensive being rich." He got out an industrial-size checkbook, scribbled in it, tore off a check, and slid it across the desk.

Jacob looked at it. "Ira, this is too generous. It's a paperback thriller, not *Gone with the Wind*."

"You got movie money coming, don't forget. The Battle of the Boobs can't go on forever. Name the kid after your Uncle Ira if it bothers you."

"What if it's a girl?"

"Irene's swell with me."

"I'll have to take it up with Ellen. You may wind up settling for a box of Havanas."

"How *is* the little woman?"

"Not so little. Everyone thinks it's twins. She's got a progressive doctor; he made her quit smoking. That hasn't improved her temperament."

"So how come you're grinning?"

"Am I? I thought I'd sprained my face."

"Well, why not? You got a family to go home to. Think of me rattling around my empty house."

"Which one, the one on Park Avenue or the one in Miami?"

"So what're you, a pinko?"

"Thanks, Ira." He put away the check. "Coming to the house-warming Saturday?"

"Wouldn't miss it, even if I do have to change trains twice. You artistic types get me: Make your killing in Manhattan, you can't wait to move out to Possum Holler."

"I feel like someone built a house on my bladder," Ellen said. "Thanks for asking."

Jacob, setting out glasses and bottles on their makeshift bar, watched her filling table lighters with fluid. "Sure you're up to a party?"

"Anything to take my mind off my hemorrhoids."

Phil Scarpetti was first to arrive, with a bottle of champagne. The artist had put on a tie for the occasion, with a plaid flannel shirt and his least paint-spotted pair of jeans. Ellen smiled brightly. "If it's okay, I'll put it in the fridge for when I can join you."

"My mother drank a six-pack a week all the time she was carrying me," Scarpetti said. "I turned out okay, if you overlook the armed-robbery thing."

Robin Elk had sent his regards from London, where he was visiting his father. Ira came with a stuffed panda bigger than he was. Cliff Cutter and his wife, Nayoka, brought a quilt she'd sewn, with good-luck tribal signs, and Alice and Howard from the office contributed a toaster. Jacob asked when they were tying the knot.

"September," said Alice. "My parents were married in September, and they're still together."

Nayoka asked Alice her favorite color. Cliff said, "She's already making that quilt in her head."

The house was in Freeport: One of a row shaped like Velveeta boxes, divided by unpaved streets named Sycamore, Weeping Willow, Elm, Oak, and Maple.

"I haven't seen a tree since I got off the train," Scarpetti said.

Jacob said, "They cut them all down to build houses."

"You should've saved the wood to make furniture."

The chairs, sofa, and table they'd brought from the apartment looked sparse in the larger setting.

"No dice." Jacob handed him a whiskey sour. "I'll need it when we start paying for the stuff we ordered from the catalogue."

The women were in the kitchen, putting cold cuts on a tray. Johnnie Ray sang on the radio.

Scarpetti asked who else was coming.

"This is it," Jacob said. "I thought of inviting Hank Stratton, but Ellen was sure he'd bring one of his tramps."

"Why in hell would you ask that blowhard?"

"I felt sorry for him. His show got canceled. Sponsors bailed. The Catholic Legion of Decency made too much noise about TV violence. Robin's thinking of letting him go. He doesn't need Lash Logan anymore."

"Good news, speaking of Hollywood." Ira stirred his rum-and-Coke with a plastic swizzle. "Unions signed an armistice."

"How?" Jacob asked.

"When the falsies are made of cotton, it's Wardrobe. When they're rubber it's Makeup."

Howard Belknap laughed, his face reddening. He was drinking straight Coca-Cola; the bachelor party had cured him of anything stronger.

Jacob asked Ira when *The Fence* was shooting.

"Right away. They got to work fast. Victor Mature has an appointment for a toga-fitting at MGM in June: He's playing the entire Roman Army. You can tell Ellen to make the bedroom suite mahogany and pay for it in cash."

Scarpetti raised his glass. "Here's to crime."

The telephone rang. "Our first call." Jacob got up to answer it. "Figures," he said, holding it out to Ira.

"I left this number. Maybe Stalin blew up the Chrysler Building." He turned his back on the others to take the call.

Howard said, "Alice loves your place. I'll have to ask Mr. Elk for a raise."

"You'll get it." Jacob drank Scotch. "I heard Paramount signed Joel McCrea for *Pistols West*. Congratulations, Cliff."

Cutter sipped rye. "They're shooting in the Arizona desert. My story takes place in Denver."

Scarpetti asked if he was going to watch the filming.

"Nayoka pestered me into it. She's got relatives on the reservation. I'll be in the saloon when they need me."

Ira hung up and sat down. He took a long drink from his glass.

"Why so glum, chum?" Scarpetti said. "Ma Bell lose a point?"

"I wish. Bad news comes after good. That was Elk's lawyer. He just talked to Elk in England, and Elk told him to call all the writers' agents in his stable."

"He better not have used that word," Cutter said. "I shovel horseshit. I don't live in it."

"What is it, Ira?" Jacob said.

"The Honorable Margery St. John got her wish. Congress is appointing a committee to investigate the paperback book industry."

"I thought you said she was sunk."

"Those kneelers getting *Lash Logan* off the air put them on the prod. Washington doesn't like being upstaged by a bunch of prissy old ladies in picture hats. Hearings begin this October. We can all expect to be subpoenaed before they're finished."

Howard blinked. "Even me?"

"I hope so, kid. One look at that freckled face and they'll drop the whole thing. You don't get votes pushing around Henry Aldrich on TV coast-to-coast."

"Gosh."

"Not to worry. Everybody gets his time on the rack: Joyce, Lawrence, Miller. It's our turn. In the end, a congressman gets to be a senator, or a Supreme Court justice, and everything goes back the way it was. Meanwhile it's just a pain in the neck."

"So's lynching." Scarpetti drained his glass.

CHAPTER
THIRTY

The House Select Committee on Pornography and Juvenile Delinquency convened in Washington in October 1951, and heard opening remarks by Margery St. John, the chairman:

"Events of the past several years have brought to the attention of this committee the necessity to identify and isolate a disturbing trend in the publishing industry.

"As a public servant, this is my sworn duty. As a widow and mother, it is my moral obligation to search out the sources of this threat and bring them under control.

"We will begin with smut.

"A decade is brief in terms of time, yet in the past ten years we have fought and won a world war, split the atom, set our sights upon the conquest of outer space—and seen a deluge of filth spill directly from the printing press into our children's bedrooms. In my opinion, some of the worst offenses against decency have taken place in the cheap publications called 'pocket books,' with the dismal implication that those wares which were once sold from seedy back rooms wrapped in brown paper to mature adults are now so small and lightweight that they may be concealed in the hip pockets and purses of impressionable youngsters, where parental supervision is difficult if not impossible. I ask, is this postwar progress, or a serious challenge to the future we will one day hand over to our children?"

"Portable porn," Jacob said. "What a concept."

Ellen, breastfeeding the baby, shushed him. On the twelve-inch screen, Representative St. John turned to a fresh page.

She was a pudgy forty, dressed like a frumpy *hausfrau* in an oatmeal-colored sweater, a knitted scarf, and owlish glasses. The camouflage was a failure. Next to her colleagues, seated behind pitchers and tumblers of water and bulky microphones, wattle-necked men in comb-overs, she looked almost glamorous.

The committee counselor, Brian P. Castor, was the youngest person present. He wore his dark hair to his collar, slicked back from a high forehead, and seemed to like his suits patterned and his neckties jazzy. The top half of his face was almost handsome, but he had a weak chin and his small mouth was placed too close to his nose. He never spoke except to address Mrs. St. John with a hand cupped over her microphone.

"Eve, meet Serpent," Jacob muttered. "Serpent, Eve."

"Jake, shut up!"

He looked at her. "You, too? Hollywood shelved *The Fence*. The last royalties didn't cover the loan I got from Ira. We're in hock up to our eyeballs, and all because a bunch of politicians want their kissers on camera."

"Patience. So far it's only campaign rhetoric."

"This is just the prologue. They'll start with friendly witnesses. We public enemies will get our turn, after sentence is passed."

"Keep your voice down. Mildred's asleep finally."

They'd named her after Ellen's mother; *Irene* was never a serious contender. He called her Millie. She had her mother's eyes and nose, and tragically her father's rat trap mouth, but her hair was coming in fair like Ellen's. He tried to picture her at age sixteen, smuggling a copy of *Guns of Gotham* into the house. Would she have him sign it?

The first witnesses called were as predicted: A baby-faced Baptist minister from Dayton, Ohio, who had gained national recognition when he hosted a comic-book burning in his church parking lot; a child psychologist from Oregon, whose authoritative German accent had been heard in an expert capacity testifying in juvenile delinquency trials in thirty-seven states; a Boston book-seller named Persons, who'd opened a carton of books he'd ordered from the Wombat Press, saw they were paperbacks, and sent them back unexamined; a series of schoolteachers from scattered districts who'd noted a disturbing change in certain students' classroom conduct between sixth and seventh grades—after they'd written reports on what they did during summer vacation and mentioned reading paperback novels; a convict serving twenty years in Atlanta for bank robbery (accompanied by a federal marshal), claiming he got his M.O. from Hugh Brock's *Mobsters from Mars*; and a grieving middle-aged woman wearing a dead fox around her throat, whose teenage son had been shot to death fleeing a candy-store robbery, and in whose bedroom she'd found a veritable crime library under the mattress.

"Ell," Jacob said, "if I'm arrested, please throw away all those complimentary books I got from Elk."

She shook her head. "And get myself arrested for tampering with evidence? You're on your own, Dillinger."

It seemed funny then.

"We need to talk, old boy."

Jacob lowered the receiver, sighed, raised it. "Robin, those are the four scariest words in the language."

"Nothing so alarming. I only want to suggest some changes in *Coal-Blooded Murder*."

"I hope it's the title. I called it *Philly Girl*. You said it sounded like the story of a horse. You underestimated the spelling skills of the reading public."

"Lunch at the club. Tomorrow at one?"

"Make it O'Hara's Grill. I always come away from the Staghunters wanting to shoot a redcoat."

The restaurant, walking distance from Blue Devil, purported to be an Irish pub. There were tankards on display and a dartboard. Jacob ordered corned beef, cabbage, and Guinness on tap.

Elk frowned at the menu and asked for scrambled eggs and a vodka martini.

"Who is that man singing?" He tilted his head in the direction of the tenor voice issuing from a loudspeaker.

"Dennis Day. What changes are we discussing?"

"Let's wait until our drinks arrive."

Scarier words yet.

When the drinks came, Elk sipped, put down his glass, and touched his lips with a silk handkerchief. "I'm concerned with just one character in the book."

"Which one?"

"Micah Rudd."

"Ah."

"'Ah' means what?"

"'Aha!' in English. He's only the main character. Is it the name? It means 'Like unto the Lord.'"

"It's not the name, but his behavior."

"You were fine with it when you read it."

"It's just that he's so—well, *aggressive* is the term that comes to mind. You catch my drift."

"No, Robin, I don't."

The blond bland features twisted into a rictus.

"You're being difficult on purpose. He's so—so—"

"Radical?"

The face went smooth. "The very term I sought. I should know better than to bandy words with a writer."

"What's radical about a coal miner asking for humane treatment from his boss? Seven fellow workers suffocated because of inadequate ventilation. Rudd warns the owner the men might strike if he refuses to discuss improvements. He has no part in the riot. My God, Robin! Rudd's not Robespierre; he's Thomas Jefferson."

"You see, that's just the thing. If Jefferson were alive today, he'd be summoned before Congress."

Their meals arrived. Jacob shoved his plate away and ordered a double Scotch.

"What do you suggest I do?"

Elk became lively.

"I hoped you'd ask. Suppose you shift the aggressive activity to a disgruntled miner with a personal grudge against the owners? It's *he* who pushes for the strike. I foresee a physical confrontation—the obstreperous laborer being the aggressor—ending in victory for Rudd as the voice of reason. The mine owner, after civilized discussion, agrees to the improvements, and everyone's the victor."

"The owner's the villain!"

Elk poked at his eggs.

"Jack—"

"Jacob."

"Jacob, I don't see how we can publish *Coal-Blooded Murder* without the changes I suggested."

Jacob drank, to tamp down the response he wanted to make.

"I'd like Phil Scarpetti to be in on this discussion," he said. "He's already submitted preliminary sketches for the cover."

Elk smiled; an uncomfortable expression on his face at the best of times.

"Mr. Scarpetti is no longer employed at Blue Devil."

"What?"

"It was his decision, although I confess it was not met without some expression of relief from the executive end."

CHAPTER
THIRTY-ONE

"*You're* the executive end, Robin. What are you trying to say?"

"He hasn't been subpoenaed yet, and I pray he won't be. But as long as he was employed here, he posed a danger. These are perilous times, Jack. Not like the war, with everyone pulling together. It's every man for himself."

It didn't occur to him to remind Elk to call him Jacob. "You're not making any sense. What do you mean by a danger?"

"You're aware he's a Marxist?"

"I am not. I don't think he has any politics at all."

"That's reason enough for Mrs. St. John's committee to suspect him. Those Yanks think anyone who doesn't wear an American flag pin in his lapel is a potential Russian spy."

"Blue Devil can survive that. He'll just tell them he doesn't belong to the Communist Party."

"You said he was dabbling in explosives the first time you met; a certain construction can be placed on that."

"He was blowing up paint, not people. He had a permit. They don't hand those out to the Rosenbergs. When did politics come into this? I thought sex was the enemy."

"That's the other thing."

"What other thing?"

The publisher groped for his cane and spun the crook.

"I wish we could have this conversation another time."

"*I* think you'd rather not have it at all."

"I thought that was obvious."

"Well, we're having it. What's the second black mark?"

"It has to do with his personal conduct."

"Oh, come on! He rubs people the wrong way. It's the artistic temperament. You said something about it yourself when you showed me his cover painting for *Chinese Checkers*. I got the impression you wouldn't have him any other way."

"I wasn't referring to his demeanor. It's his private life the committee will want to explore."

"You mean his homosexuality."

"You knew?"

"I suspected it for some time. My bachelor party more or less confirmed it. He dumped her off his lap as if she were a cat and he had allergies. It still doesn't make him a Commie."

"The committee's main interest is perversion. They'll say his images send a subtle message to the impressionable younger generation—recruitment posters, as it were."

"All his female models are knockouts and half-naked. Sometimes more than half. Wouldn't that send a mixed message to fledgling fairies?"

"You may have noticed his women are always either up to something nefarious or are themselves victims of a hairy he-man. His pictures are a misogynist's dream."

"If you feel that way, why'd you hire him?"

"I was thinking of sales. I believe it was William Randolph Hearst who said, 'Show me a magazine with a dog, a baby, or a pretty girl on the cover, and I'll show you a magazine that sells.' I'd alter that to read, 'a pretty girl in her knickers.' Jack, we're all going to have to pull in our horns if we don't want to end up on trial. Fewer naughty bits on the cover, more subtlety on the page. You're a good enough writer to embrace this opportunity."

"'Opportunity'?"

"It's an ill wind, etcetera. Some of the finest art has appeared in times of oppression. Da Vinci flowered under the Borgias. In our own time, Hollywood censorship forced clever screenwriters and directors to exploit subterfuge and innuendo to make their point, with even greater impact. You're up to the task. Hank Stratton is not; his hardcover deal fell through when his television program was canceled. His agent came to me asking for a new contract, on far more modest terms than the last. I turned him down. Stratton swats flies with Howitzers. The committee would rip him to shreds and us with him."

"I never liked Stratton, but he deserves better. His sales are what put this hobby of yours over the top."

Elk tried to look sly; the effect was more like a baby who'd soiled a fresh diaper.

"Just between us, dear fellow, his numbers were never as reported. His work offended critics, leading to notoriety, which I finessed into figures no one ever bothered to investigate. Lash Logan brought us sensation. *Chinese Checkers* was our very first title to sell through."

"My God. You've got more twists and turns than a snake. How did the Krauts ever manage to shoot you down?"

Elk took this as a compliment. His milk-pale cheeks stained pink.

"This crisis will blow over. Soon the watchdogs of morality will find a juicier target: Comic books and television are ripe for the plucking. Why pillory artists and writers whose faces are unknown when you can go after Lucille Ball and get your picture on the front page?"

"So meanwhile we bend over and grab our ankles."

"What a vulgar way of putting it; but, yes, figuratively speaking. This too shall pass."

Elk fell on his meal as if he'd been living on coconuts on a desert island. Jacob let his own grow cold.

"The old clichés are the best," he said. "If Scarpetti goes, so do I."

"You can't."

"I'm sorry?"

"You're under contract for another book, and if I decide *Coal-Blooded Murder* is unsatisfactory—should you withhold unreasonably the changes I suggest—you'll owe me two. If you try to change publishers, I'll take you to court."

"You're threatening me."

"Certainly not. You're more than a colleague, Jack. This is advice from a friend."

"Not Jack! Jacob! You don't know what a friend is. You'd throw your mother under the train just to show your old man you can wipe your own ass."

"Another crudity. Shall we part as adversaries?"

"Let's just part." He rose and put money on the table.

"Put that away. The publisher always picks up the check."

"I'm not sure you're my publisher anymore."

"You weren't listening to what I said."

"Believe it or not, Robin, there are other professions besides writing."

"As I recall, your last job came with a foreman."

"People who work for foremen don't get called up before Congress." He left.

CHAPTER
THIRTY-TWO

Ellen frowned. She seemed to be concentrating on trimming Millie's nails.

That had surprised Jacob the day she gave birth. He'd had no idea babies came with nails that needed paring. But although she was being careful she wasn't entirely focused on the chore. The girl, for her part, lay on the changing table looking all around the room without squirming.

"You're sure that's how you left it?" Ellen said. "You didn't say anything you couldn't take back?"

"I was cowardly enough not to."

"That wasn't being a coward. That was being a responsible father. If it were just us, it'd be different. We could let the house go and find a cheap apartment. But it isn't just us, is it?"

"A little baby sure takes up a lot of space."

"She takes up the whole world."

"Still, I can't help feeling I betrayed Phil."

"He'll find something. Artists who like boys aren't exactly whooping cranes."

"That's harsh."

"I didn't mean it to be. He only has to support himself."

"I have to tell him I didn't leave Blue Devil in a huff before he finds out on his own."

"Call him."

"It's a talk that has to take place in person."

"Do you think that's a good idea?"

"What's bad about it?"

"He might have been subpoenaed by now. The FBI or somebody may be watching his place."

"So what? Is visiting a friend against the law now?"

"They could think you're like him."

"I'm married. I've got a kid!"

She shook her head. "You're still a country boy at heart. It's one of the reasons I fell in love with you." She tickled Millie, laughed when she laughed, and went up on her toes to kiss Jacob. Her eyes were grave. "Do what you feel you have to do, but remember: It isn't just you."

Phil Scarpetti opened his door. His expression was no more sour than usual. "I see by your face you're wise."

"Elk told me. I'm sorry."

"Me, too, about *Coal-Blooded Murder*. I'd show you my sketches, but they'd just depress you. Best I've ever done."

Jacob smelled pot. "You think that's a good idea?"

"Tell you what. I'll go ahead and paint the thing, give it to you for your first anniversary."

"I mean smoking reefers. Elk would count it another nail in your coffin."

Scarpetti stepped aside for him to enter.

"Drink? I'd offer you a toke, but I don't want to get you in Dutch with J. Edgar Hoover."

"A little early for me, but don't go dry on my account."

The artist threw himself full length on his sofa and crossed his ankles. He was in his stocking feet and his favorite paint-stained shirt hung outside his trousers. "Alcohol would be an insult to the great god Cannabis. Why the long face? Look at the portfolio I'm putting together." He waved a hand around the apartment, which was cluttered as always. Cast-off clothing and dirty coffee cups shared the space with partial paintings on easels. The color scheme was dark, the sinister subjects lacking the usual irony.

"Kind of grim."

"I was getting stale. Past due for a shake-up." He watched Jacob take a seat. "Hey, you didn't do something stupid like quit Elk, did you?"

"I tried. He reminded me I have a contract."

"He tried to get me to sign one once, but I hate leashes. Not one of my smarter moments; but like I said, it's time to do something else. I'm not even sure I want to go on painting. Trouble is I'm not prepared for anything else except armed robbery, and I stunk at it."

"Maybe *I* should try it. Who knows? I might have a talent."

"Stop talking like an idiot."

"I was about to tell you the same thing," Jacob said. "You were born to paint. Make the rounds of galleries. There's no reason Norman Rockwell should get all the work."

"Maybe when I get the time."

"From the look of you, you've got plenty."

Scarpetti took a fold of paper from a shirt pocket and tossed it in his visitor's lap.

The document was printed in archaic letters on stiff paper, ending with the line: "Herein fail not."

"You've been subpoenaed."

"Yeah. Dig the lingo. The monkey who delivered it should've worn tights and carried a trumpet."

"Do you have a lawyer?"

"No. I'm out of work, remember?"

"Maybe I can help."

"When Hollywood gets around to shooting *The Fence*, I'll take all you've got. Nobody's telling little Dixie her Uncle Phil ate up her college fund."

"Millie."

"You're stopping at one kid?"

"Do yourself a favor and leave that sense of humor outside the hearing room. Those vultures are just waiting for an excuse to rip into somebody like you."

Scarpetti took a deep drag, blew smoke out his nostrils, and reached behind his head to drop the roach in the ashtray.

"What do you mean, 'somebody like you'?"

"Do I need to spell it out?"

"Yeah, pal. I think you do."

"Phil, I'm on your side."

"I'd prefer you up my ass."

"Jesus!"

The artist's grin was vicious.

"Just kidding, Jake. I'm strictly supply side. The boys downtown call me Phil Spaghetti, on account of the size of my meatballs."

"Go ahead, get it out of your system before they fly you to Washington."

"Elk told you I'm a fag, didn't he?"

"He tried every way not to."

"Oh. I get it. Didn't know I was that obvious."

"You're not. But good friends aren't much for keeping secrets. Phil, I don't give a shit if you're John Wayne or Tinker Bell. You're my friend and I came over to make sure you're all right."

"Don't worry. As far as the committee's concerned, you and I just worked together. They can't lynch you for hanging out with a sissy at the office."

"You think I care about that? If they don't send for me I'll volunteer to be your character witness."

"Don't perjure yourself on my account."

It was no use. Jacob stood. "I'll talk to you sometime when you're not high."

"Good luck. Elk gave me a month's severance and I know a doorman who can keep me in muggles for a month."

"Phil—"

He reached behind his head, groped for the still-smoldering joint, and took a hit. "Go back home and work on making that Dixie."

———

Jacob intended to walk as far as he could, but after a few blocks he boarded the subway. For the first time, the buzzing city had failed to calm him.

He opened his door and read Ellen's face.

"It came, didn't it?" he said.

PART FOUR

1951

DIME A DOZEN

CHAPTER
THIRTY-THREE

Gilbert Ter Horst resembled a professional wrestler. His head was naked skull and sat square on his shoulders without benefit of a neck. Although his suit was cut to his measure, the way he stood to shake hands, in a sort of crouch, suggested he'd look more at home in tights.

He specialized in Constitutional law.

"I'll be honest, Mr. Ter Horst," Jacob said. "We can't afford you. I swallowed my pride and asked Robin Elk if the firm's lawyer would take my case, but he said it would be a conflict of interest."

"Of course he did. It means if things look bad for the company, he intends to shift the blame to you."

Ellen gripped Jacob's hand with one of hers wearing a white cotton glove. "I can't believe that of Robin," she said. "He's always been a gentleman."

They sat facing the lawyer's desk in his office overlooking Central Park. The room was done in copper and leather.

"Gentlemen don't last long in a hearing room, Mrs. Heppleman. Don't worry about my fee. I've waited for this case. We'll work out a payment plan we can all live with."

Jacob said, "Forty a year for forty years would be ideal. We had to take out a loan to pay the babysitter."

"Hang on to that sense of humor. You'll need it. Do you know what to expect?"

"We've been watching the hearings on TV."

"So far the witnesses have all been friendly to the government's case. It will be far different when the representatives and their attorney take the gloves off."

"Can I invoke the Fifth Amendment?"

"You can try, but if the committee doesn't agree the answers would be self-incriminating, they'll jail you for contempt. They have the advantage of a gray area in the First Amendment."

"I wasn't aware it had one. I read up on the Bill of Rights after the subpoena came. It seemed pretty specific."

"It can be interpreted a variety of ways. There are exceptions, such as yelling 'fire' in a crowded theater, and any police officer can arrest you for public profanity. In recent years such exceptions have been expanded to include pornography, but since Congress hasn't the authority to enforce laws, the argument can be made that you won't be incriminating yourself."

"My God," Jacob said. "That's Kafkaesque."

"There's also the possibility you could be charged with contributing to the delinquency of minors, but that's a fight I can win. Writing a scurrilous book and handing a teenager a loaded revolver aren't the same thing.

"On one hand," he went on, "they're saying the right of free speech doesn't cover the dissemination of prurient material, while on the other they're saying it does, and therefore no laws have been broken—for their purposes."

"Scratch Kafka. That's Orwellian."

"I'd counsel you against using literary allusions on the stand. They'll think you're pompous and turn up the heat." He looked at Ellen. "Will you be attending?"

"I don't think we can afford it. The government is only paying Jacob's expenses."

"Try. It makes a good impression when the witness's loyal wife is sitting behind him; the cameras pick her up whenever they cut to the testimony. It helps that you're attractive; but not *too* attractive."

"Thanks. I think."

"Don't be offended. Too much glamour sends a carnal message rather than a domestic one. Dress nice; but dress down, and go easy on the powder and paint."

Jacob said, "She'll be sitting behind me? Are the seats assigned?"

"You let me worry about that."

"Mr. Ter Horst," he said, "are you going to bribe a page?"

"An incentive. They're not public officials." He opened a drawer in the desk and pushed a dog-eared paperback across the blotter with the cover facing up. It was the movie edition of *The Fence*. "Will you sign it?"

"You're a fan?"

"My wife found it under our son's mattress. We joked about shipping him off to military school. Then I read it. I'm no judge of literature, but it's hard to put down, and based on what I've heard from my colleagues in criminal law, quite accurate as to detail." His smile was abashed. "It fell right open to the scene depicted on the cover."

Ellen, blushing, murmured to Jacob: "I'm so glad Phil replaced me with Grace Kelly."

His testimony was scheduled for January 1952. He spent two months being mock-interrogated by Ter Horst, who shed his office manners to assume the role of a member of the House Select Committee on Pornography and Juvenile Delinquency. Jacob wondered if he rehearsed his bully act in private.

"Mr. Heppleman, would you tell us which of your books you'd recommend to someone unfamiliar with your work?"

"I suppose that would be *Katt's Alley*."

"Not *Chinese Checkers*? I believe that was your first."

"It was good enough at the time I wrote it, but my work has improved a great deal since then."

"I should hope so. I read *Chinese Checkers*. Can you tell us what *Katt's Alley* is about?"

"It's about a teenage tough named Billy Katt, whose gangland empire occupies the alley behind his apartment house. He sells drugs, leads brawls against rival gangs, sexually assaults a female prep-school student, and shoots himself in the head when the police come to arrest him."

"And you consider this an improvement over your earlier work?"

"It's a cautionary tale."

"But the young man doesn't really pay for his crimes, does he?"

"I'm sorry. I thought I said he committed suicide."

"But that's closer to divine intervention than the right and proper exercise of law enforcement by officials sworn to keep the peace, is it not?"

"I don't understand, Congressman. I—"

"Congresswoman."

He grimaced. "How was I to know you're Mrs. St. John now? You were Roger Wellborn of Massachusetts last time."

"Don't break character. What don't you understand, Mr. Heppleman?"

"The boy put a bullet in his skull. It wasn't God with His finger on the trigger. What's the difference, so long as he paid for his poor choices? It would prevent most young people from making the same mistakes."

"I fail to see how. They would just shrug and say they won't shoot themselves. Can you tell us about the warehouse burglary?"

"What warehouse burglary?"

"Can it be that I'm more familiar with your work than you are, or have you committed so many sins against decency you can't keep them all straight?"

"I object."

Ter Horst smiled. "That's my job, although I won't be exercising it as often as I'm sure you'd like. It loses its edge through repetition." He switched personalities again. "I'm referring to the warehouse burglary in *Katt's Alley*. Not only do you provide a detailed plan of the crime, but your publisher saw fit to diagram it on the back cover. Frankly, this strikes me as a primer for crime."

"I made up the warehouse. It doesn't exist. The plan was a product of my imagination. I've never robbed a warehouse."

"And you don't consider this contributing to the delinquency of minors."

"Excuse me, Congresswoman, but is that a question?"

"Counselor," Ter Horst corrected. "Now I'm Brian P. Castor, attorney to the committee."

"Is that necessary? In the hearing room I'll know who's asking the questions."

"Would you rather I made the rehearsal easier than the real thing, or harder? Answer the question."

"Counselor, I would never consider contributing to the delinquency of a minor. I have an infant daughter."

"And when your daughter is, say, age thirteen; would you recommend she read *Katt's Alley?*"

"Why not? I'd like her to know what her old man does for a living and whether he's any good at it."

"Mr. Heppleman, you and I differ significantly in our interpretation of what's good."

"Who are you now?" Jacob said.

"Does it matter?"

He came home from these sessions wrung out, with no energy to make the rewrites Elk had insisted on in *Coal-Blooded Murder.* He fought with Ellen, shouted at Millie when she wouldn't stop crying. He drank more. Many nights he passed out in his chair in front of the TV test pattern.

Ellen and Millie moved out after the first month.

"Not permanently, Jake. This isn't the environment for Mildred. Call me at Mom's when you want to get together. But not when you're moody or drunk. That isn't the environment for *me.*"

"You said you'd stay by my side through this."

"I'll give you encouragement when you need it, and I'll be in the hearing room. Mom can look after Mildred while we're in Washington."

"Without you here, things will just get worse."

"Don't act like you have no choice. You're an adult, not one of the kids who sneak your books into their rooms."

"Now you sound like Ter Horst trying to sound like the literature police. This is a nightmare."

She smiled and took both his hands in hers. She had on her traveling suit, which fit her again at last. She'd been working out with Jack LaLanne on television.

"They can't do anything to you, dear. It isn't as if you ever actually broke the law."

CHAPTER
THIRTY-FOUR

In January, a face jumped out at Jacob from page six of *The Greenwich Clock*. The flat features and protruding eyes looked even more grotesque in a police mug shot than they did in person. It was the first time he'd seen him without a hat: His dull, nappy hair clung to his skull like the felt on a pool table. The headline read:

UNDERWORLD'S "MERCHANT OF MENACE" GETS LIFE
Ice pick killer henchman turns state's evidence to beat Death Row

Jacob read the short article without emotion. Not so long ago, Irish Mickey Shannon behind bars would have brought him relief, but now a vengeful government with a piece of paper seemed almost as terrifying as a dwarf with a pistol.

Page two was more compelling. The tabloid had begun covering the hearings of the House Select Committee on Pornography and Juvenile Delinquency in a close-printed column that resembled the shipping news. It was a combination digest of the proceedings and box score, with forthcoming witnesses listed at the bottom. Philip N. Scarpetti was slated to testify on the fourteenth.

The paper's (i.e. Sam Rosetti's) stand was clear. A sidebar, bordered in black like a death notice, quoted Rep. St. John's opening remarks from the first day of the third week of the hearings:

Ten years ago, this kind of literature was not easily obtained in this hemisphere: One had to visit certain disreputable neighborhoods in Paris, France, and smuggle it home in a plain brown wrapper. I assumed, naïvely, that it could never be popular in America. But judging by sales figures and the proliferation of these two-bit presses since the end of the war, I must conclude that something drastic happened to us over there, and that we lost something we may never get back.

His respect for the congresswoman from Nebraska went up a notch. The naïveté, of course, was in thinking there had never been a pornography industry in the western world; but ten years ago, the speaker had been Mrs. St. John, housewife, and unlikely to visit the shops where such material was available in her own backyard. He understood her bereavement for the loss of innocence. Her mistake was in trying to turn back the clock.

———

"State your full name for the record, please."

"Philip Nunzio Scarpetti."

Margery St. John did most of the questioning; *why* became apparent as Jacob and Ellen watched the televised interrogation. She was the only woman on the committee.

"You are a professional illustrator, is that correct?"

"No, ma'am."

"From—pardon me, did you say 'no'?"

"Yes, ma'am."

"You're not a professional illustrator?"

"No, ma'am. I'm unemployed at present."

"But your profession is illustration?"

"Yes, ma'am."

"I appreciate your politeness, Mr. Scarpetti, but I prefer to be addressed as either 'Congresswoman' or 'Representative.'"

"I'll try to remember that, Congresswoman."

"From 1946 until last year you were employed by Blue Devil Books to illustrate its covers, were you not?"

"I was, Congresswoman."

Scarpetti's dark complexion washed out under the harsh lights. He wore a checked sportcoat over a pale shirt and dark tie. Jacob had never seen him look so respectable. His responses were calm, but his Adam's apple worked after each question and before each answer. He sat alone behind the microphone on the witnesses' table, no lawyer in sight.

St. John nodded at someone out of frame. The cameras panned to a pull-down screen set up in a corner of the big room visible to the committee and spectators. A slide made from a blowup photo of a Blue Devil cover appeared: A woman in a torn slip strapped to a tilted operating table faced forward, her expression a rictus of fear. In the foreground, in three-quarter view facing her, a leering man in a white lab coat brandished a scalpel.

"Let the record show this is a reproduction of the cover of a book titled *Dr. Sadisto*, by Hugh Brock," said St. John. "Mr. Scarpetti, did you paint this cover?"

"Do I have to answer that?"

"Are you invoking your Fifth Amendment right to avoid self-incrimination?"

"No, I'm embarrassed to own up to that painting. I was pretty crude in the beginning. The answer is yes."

"Crude, as opposed to now?" She nodded again.

A new slide shuttled into place. A woman, naked but with certain body parts camouflaged by cactus, was staked spread-eagle on a desert floor, staring bug-eyed at a savage Indian standing over her, wearing only a breechcloth.

"Let the record show this is a reproduction of a book titled *Cry Comanche*, by Cliff Cutter. Did you paint this cover, Mr. Scarpetti?"

"Yes, ma—Congresswoman, I did. I'm kind of proud of the chiaroscuro. It's hard to pull off and still get the effect of blazing sun and searing heat."

192 · Loren D. Estleman

"This isn't an art class, Mr. Scarpetti. Next."

Jacob cringed. It was *Chinese Checkers*. The Asian girl looked five times as menacing and her male victim ten times more exposed in the blowup.

"Mr. Scarpetti—"

"Yes, Congresswoman. I painted it."

More slides followed: P. B. Collier's *Teen-Age Tramp*, Arthur Burt's *Riddle of the Sands*, Hank Stratton's *Strumpet Street*, *The Fence*, by Jack Holly.

Ellen groaned. It was the original version, with the half-dressed woman undoubtedly inspired by her.

"Mr. Scarpetti?"

"Sorry, Congresswoman. I was admiring my work. I had to revise it for the movie edition, but I prefer this one."

"Is that all you have to say about it?"

"To say anything more would be immodest."

"Has it struck you your work has a recurring theme?"

"No. That is to say, it would be no great revelation. Blue Devil specializes in suspense fiction, so there has to be an element of danger on every cover."

"I'm speaking of the subject matter. In every cover we've shown—and many we haven't time to show—a woman is either in mortal peril or placing a man in that situation. These women are invariably in a state of undress. Does this tableau represent your views of the sex?"

"Those scenes were written by others. I only illustrated them."

"Mr. Scarpetti, the members of this committee are aware of the contents of these books. In almost all the scenes you chose to paint, the women were fully clothed. In some cases, those scenes don't even exist. Is your opinion of women so low that you can only depict them as either depraved predators or victims of rape?"

"Every member of the committee has read each book?"

"What is your point?"

"It just seems like a massive waste of government time and the taxpayers' money."

Roger Wellborn of Massachusetts spoke. "Are you attempting to lecture to this committee?"

"Far from it, Congressman. But as a taxpayer myself, I think I deserve an accounting."

Counselor Castor covered St. John's microphone with a hand and whispered something in her ear.

"To clarify," said she, when the hand withdrew, "congressional aides read the books and provided the committee with detailed summaries of the plots. Answer the question, please."

"The answer is no. I have no opinion of women, low or high."

"Is it your observation that readers of the books you illustrate have a low opinion of women?"

"That's not my job. I painted what I was paid to paint."

"Are you married, Mr. Scarpetti?"

"No, Congresswoman. I'm a bachelor."

"A confirmed bachelor?"

His Adam's apple bobbed, but his voice remained steady. "I wouldn't say confirmed. It's just a fact of life."

"You were convicted of armed robbery in 1941, is that correct?"

"It is."

"You stole a bottle of whiskey from a pharmacy, then re-entered the store and attempted to rob the pharmacist at knife point; is that correct?"

"It is."

"And you were sentenced to serve ten years in the New York State Penitentiary in Ossining?"

"Is that a question?"

"Answer it, please."

"I wasn't evading the question, Congresswoman. It sounded like a statement. I was released after four years for good behavior. I've been law-abiding ever since."

"During those four years, did you know a convict named Charles Winthrop?"

"Yes. He taught me to draw and paint."

"Is that all he taught you?"

He hesitated. "I don't understand the question, Congress-woman."

"Are you sure?"

Ellen's hand clenched Jacob's hard enough to hurt.

Scarpetti said, "I can't answer a question I don't understand."

"Very well. I'll spell it out. Mr. Winthrop served twelve years for statutory rape. When a man who can't control his primal urges is forced to spend many years in the exclusive company of men—"

Scarpetti scraped back his chair and stood.

"What are you doing?"

"Leaving."

"You haven't been dismissed."

"I'm dismissing myself."

"I warn you, Mr. Scarpetti, you're in danger of being incarcerated for contempt of Congress."

"Well put. Good-bye, ma'am."

"Sergeant-at-arms, please take Mr. Scarpetti into custody."

Jacob got up and turned off the set. "Sometimes there's just nothing on TV you want to see," he said.

CHAPTER THIRTY-FIVE

The hotel was comfortable enough, but the staff was indifferent. When, twenty minutes after the couple checked in, Jacob called the front desk to report that the TV wasn't working, the phone rang eleven times before a bored-sounding clerk answered. Maintenance came six hours later.

Ellen's mother was too busy fighting a kitchen fire to babysit Millie back home. Mrs. Boyle, a neighbor, filled in. She was a retired midwife and a fan of the Screamer Fairfax books.

"Anyway," Ellen said, "the view's not bad."

He joined her at the window, through which they could see part of the Capitol dome. "Let's hope I don't leave it in handcuffs like Phil."

———

"Welcome to D.C. Is this your first visit?"

Ter Horst, outside the committee room, took his hand in a mighty grip, like a firefighter grasping the wrist of a man hanging off the ledge of a burning building. His shaved head reflected light from every bump and declivity.

Ellen, her tweed suit freshly cleaned and pressed, nodded. "We hope to do some sightseeing while we're here."

"If I make bail." Jacob wore his good pinstripe under a light topcoat and a hat with a brim he thought narrow, but Ellen said that was the fashion. "You don't want to look like one of those gangsters in the Kefauver hearings."

The lawyer exuded confidence from every pore. "Don't worry; they'll start easy. Feel you out."

"You mean lull me into a false sense of security."

"We've been all through it. You know what to expect. If they throw you a curve, let me take a swing at it."

The atmosphere in the vast building was like the first day of school: same ambient din of cross-conversations, same chill air, same smell of cheap floor wax.

Same fear of bullies.

He hung his coat in an open cloak room, found space for his hat in a line of them, like heads staked outside the Tower of London, and shambled on along the Last Mile.

The place was built to remind visitors of their own insignificance in the corridors of power: The ceilings even in the passages were a mile high, the stair treads so deep they made him feel like a small child tiptoeing to a floor from which he'd been banned, the size of the hearing room gargantuan despite the throngs of people who seemed crowded into it; whenever the door opened to let someone in or out, the glimpse inside made him sick at heart. Ellen snaked her arm inside his in what was no doubt an attempt to offer strength, but which felt as if she let go she'd be swept away by a riptide. He could feel her heart thud.

Or maybe it was his. He had butterflies in his stomach for the first time since combat.

Which was what this was; except he was armed only with an attorney, not a BAR he'd dismantled and put back together so often he could depend on it absolutely.

They sat in a waiting room that was possibly the smallest room in the building, but he felt naked in it. Ter Horst, seated next to him on a hard bench, smiled as Jacob fumbled out a cigarette, and offered him a light. His client had trouble keeping the cigarette in the flame.

The lawyer put away his pigskin lighter. "I didn't know you smoked."

"I don't. I didn't. But it was the only thing left to be driven to. I'm already a drunk."

"My fault," Ellen said. "I thought it would distract him from the bottle. We have a little girl, you know."

"Indubitably I do. I intend to draw her like a gun if it becomes necessary."

She glared. "You won't drag her into this."

"She won't be subpoenaed." He turned to Jacob. "You're not a defendant. They're only after publicity. No one wants to put anyone in jail. Give them a good show and they'll all be after you to ghost their memoirs."

"Tell that to Phil Scarpetti. He's locked up in Atlanta for the rest of the session. If this had happened while he was still on parole, he'd be back in Sing Sing."

"He was stupid. He should have hired an attorney, who would have stopped him from walking out. There's nothing to be gained from making these people mad."

"I tried to contact him before he packed his toothbrush. We parted badly last time and I wanted to apologize and offer encouragement. His phone number was discontinued, my letters were returned, and when I went to see him, he'd moved. He must've checked into one of those crummy hotels he's always painting."

"Embarrassed, I imagine. That 'confirmed bachelor' crack was low. It's no small thing to be exposed as a homosexual coast-to-coast."

"It wasn't that. He told me what he was. That's why we fought. He thought I was judging him and I guess I was."

"You weren't, Jakey," Ellen said. "Phil just got tired of hating himself and decided to hate you instead."

"Hates himself? He has—had—a great sense of humor."

She smiled. "You can be such a child. Don't be offended; it's one of the reasons I fell in love with you."

"I was hoping it was my rugged good looks."

Ter Horst interrupted the domestic banter.

"If it means anything, Scarpetti's the hero of the day. He did what a lot of blowhards swore they'd do, then chickened out in front of the microphone. The American Civil Liberties Union would elect him president tomorrow."

"It wouldn't mean anything to him."

Ellen patted his hand. "Stop worrying about Phil. He's a grown man, and he survived prison once. You need to concentrate on yourself."

"Excellent advice," Ter Horst said.

"This is the first time I've concentrated on anyone else since this thing started. I don't know why I'm here. All I do is write books. I'm an entertainer—I can't quite bring myself to say *author*—not a Fifth Column saboteur or a drug-pusher or even a guy who sells French postcards on a school playground. What do they want with me, anyway?"

Ter Horst got his lighter back out and lit a gold-tipped cigarette. "They don't want you at all. As far as they're concerned, you're not even small potatoes. They want what you represent. And they only want that because they can show slides of half-naked women and steal the spotlight from Adlai Stevenson and Dwight D. Eisenhower."

"I should've stayed in the army."

"No refuge there. Joe McCarthy's squawking about Communists in the armed services. Television's got eighteen hours to fill and they're running out of Charlie Chan movies. Sooner or later the viewers will get tired of looking at ugly politicians and demand more soap operas and quiz shows. We just have to wait this one out."

"Like Scarpetti," Jacob said.

The sergeant-at-arms, brush-cut and straight-backed, opened the door from the other side and called out a name. A man wearing a creased tie on a cheap cotton shirt got up from his bench and went inside. He looked like a patient going in for major surgery. The door drifted shut on the drone of voices within.

The occupants of the waiting room were a cross-section of America in *Life* magazine: Seamed-faced farmer types in Christmas ties and Sunday suits, Brilliantined used-car dealers in window-check sportcoats, librarians in buns and mannish suits, a nonde-script party in blue serge with a briefcase on his lap who might have been a CPA or a hired killer for the Mob. Jacob couldn't distinguish between the Friendly Witnesses and those who were on trial for their livelihoods; for their lives.

Ellen sensed his mounting panic. She patted his hand again. How quickly and thoroughly they all became mothers.

So far, Jacob and Phil were the only ones subpoenaed from Blue Devil; there were a dozen houses yet to be heard from, and summons-servers had only so much drive. Cliff Cutter was inac-cessible, dragging his bones through desert sage aboard a tough little mustang in quest of source material. Hugh Brock, that strange little man, had committed himself to a private mental hospital to sweat out his demons, and Phoebe Sternwalter was probably too small and frail-looking to beat up on in public. The genteel whodunits of the Burt team could hardly be blamed for the salacious covers that had bought them comfortable homes in the country (in different postal zones, needless to say).

Robin Elk had returned to England; to administer his father's affairs, he said, while the old gent was in hospital awaiting the Inevitable. There might have been some truth in the excuse, but it didn't change Jacob's opinion of him. He'd had the guts to sur-vive a German POW camp, but not to face a housewife from the Midwest.

Damn the politicians. They made cowards out of people who under other circumstances might have been heroes.

No one seemed to know what had become of Hank Strat-ton. After his TV show was canceled, two low-budget movies adapted from his books were shelved pending results of the hear-ings. Rumors ranged from voluntary service in Korea to r-and-r in a whorehouse in Nevada. Jacob couldn't fault him in either case. A blank page was frightening enough; when they took away your words, what was left?

He was putting out his third cigarette in a heavy stand when a man came in from the stairs and sat. He was slightly built in a brown suit cut for a heftier man—the knees bagged nearly to his shins—with smears of gray ash on each lapel and a burn hole in one sleeve. His clothes—weather-beaten hat, scuffed brown oxfords, a wide necktie with a hula girl painted on it—screamed pawnshop.

Pawnshop. It was like a blow from an open palm.

The man hadn't aged. He saw him as remembered, behind a high old-fashioned counter in a room stuffed with old furniture, musty books, toasters in stacks, firearms—and a glossy black Remington Streamliner portable typewriter. A twentieth-century Bob Cratchit in sleeve-protectors and a green eyeshade, with a stumpy revolver in his fist.

He shuddered.

Ellen said, "What? Someone walk over your grave?"

"Close. I just saw an old acquaintance. Linus Pickering. You wouldn't know him. I threatened him with a pistol once and threw a brick through his window."

CHAPTER
THIRTY-SIX

Next to a doctor shaking his head, a polished attorney stiffening in his seat was as disconcerting as things could get.

"I don't know how much time we have," he whispered, "so you'd better talk fast. What window?"

"It was a long time ago, and I thought we were square." As quietly as possible, he told about the typewriter in the window, his squabble with the pawnbroker, the weapons drawn, and the vandalism and theft afterward.

"Jake!" Ellen snatched away her hand.

"I made it right later, I thought. I paid for the machine and offered to cut him in on *The Fence* if he let me pick his brain for research. I came through on my promise: I don't owe him anything."

Ter Horst scowled. "If you'd cut him in on the advance from Hollywood, he probably wouldn't be here."

"What are you saying?"

"I'm saying Washington made him a better offer."

"They *pay* witnesses?"

"Not in money; at least not in a way it could be traced. But men in his line have been known to deal in stolen property. Once they're of use to authority, poof! No more outstanding warrants."

"So what do we do?"

"We profit from their mistake. They shouldn't have let you see him before you testify. They could have asked if you'd ever committed a felony and if you said no, bring him in to refuse. Then they'd slap you with everything from lying to Congress to the contributing-to-delinquency charge."

"I've been writing about the wrong bad guys."

"Hold on. Now, you'll say, 'Yes, I once committed a felony,' and explain it as you just did. It might buy you some sympathy as a recently returned veteran who regrets an error of judgment, most likely caused by the trauma of combat."

"That could work," Ellen said.

"But if this *wasn't* a mistake, and they call him first, all bets are off. It will play like you cobbled up a phony story after you got caught with your hand in the cookie jar. You're condemned before you sit down."

"What are the odds it's a mistake?"

Ter Horst's smile pulled grimly at the corners of his mouth.

"Not great; but it wouldn't be the first time a politician tripped over his own red tape."

Please, God, let me be first.

He hadn't prayed for such a thing since sandlot baseball.

Ellen pressed her hip against his.

"Whatever happens, happens," she said. "It's not in our hands."

"I'm sorry I didn't tell you. I couldn't stand the idea of you thinking I'm some kind of thug."

"Anyone can be stupid, even an honest man. We've known each other a long time, Jake. I *know* you can be stupid."

He laughed then, loud enough to draw the attention of all the people in the waiting room; including Pickering, who noticed him for the first time with a start. Jacob pretended he hadn't seen him. He wiped his eyes on his handkerchief. What she'd said wasn't that funny, but he'd kept his emotions pent up so long they burst through the first available opening.

Ter Horst grunted.

"I've had three wives. I'd trade them all for yours."

Jacob barely heard him. *Please, God, let me be first.*

The door to the hearing room opened and the sergeant-at-arms stuck out his square head. "Jacob Heppleman."

Gilbert Ter Horst smiled.

"Jack Holly, you were born under a lucky star."

CHAPTER
THIRTY-SEVEN

Mrs. St. John smiled. She was so thoroughly the suburban Betty Crocker housewife—kids splashing in mud puddles and a tuna casserole browning in the oven—that she put Jacob on his guard as if she were J. Edgar Hoover.

"Thank you for agreeing to speak to this committee, Mr. Heppleman."

He mumbled something polite in response; in thirty seconds the harsh lights of television burst pods of perspiration from all his pores. Ter Horst pressed his shoulder against his—a tiny nudge, invisible on camera.

"You served in Europe during the Second World War?"

"Yes, ma—Congresswoman."

"'Ma'am' is fine. A veteran needn't stand on ceremony."

Already she'd sorted him out from Phil Scarpetti: ex-con, painter of naked women, and a pervert to boot.

To hell with that.

"Yes, Congresswoman. I served with the twenty-third infantry."

"With distinction, I understand."

"Congresswoman, everyone over there served with distinction."

"Well put. What was your occupation before the war?"

"I spent six months loading steel coils onto trucks bound for factories in Detroit, Cleveland, and Gary, Indiana. When I left that job, I wrote for magazines."

"Commonly called the pulps, is that correct? Publications produced on rough-cut paper and offered to the public at the price of ten cents apiece?"

"That is correct."

"Did you write a story called 'Chinese Checkers'?"

He felt a sudden impish impulse to take a page from Scarpetti's book. "No, Congresswoman; I did not."

Some confusion while the members of the committee buzzed among themselves, flapping open folders and sorting through closely typed pages.

Margery St. John peered through her glasses at a document before her. "We have a photocopy of the story as it appeared in a publication titled *Double-Barreled Detective,* with your byline."

"It wasn't a story. It was a novel, serialized in five issues of the magazine."

"I fail to see the difference."

"A story appears in one issue only, and in general pays a penny a word. A serialized novel involves a legal contract, and the author receives a flat rate. I don't expect someone outside the industry to appreciate the difference, but I assure you it's profound."

Counselor Castor palmed St. John's microphone and moved his lips almost against her ear.

"We're not here to explore the inner workings of publishing, Mr. Heppleman. The purpose of these hearings is to determine the effect of stories of sordid crime upon impressionable youth, and whether they cross the line between license and licentiousness. You're the author of a book titled *The Fence,* are you not?"

"I am."

"Your main character, one Mike Moynihan, deals in illegal merchandise?"

"That's what a fence does."

"Is he based on a real person?"

He slid his eyes Ter Horst's way. The attorney, concentrating on the panel, gave him nothing back.

He leaned into the microphone. "Partially."

There might have been a murmur in the room; he wasn't sure.

"What do you mean by 'partially'?"

"Characters are usually an amalgamation of several real people and an invention of the writer's."

"Can you identify one of these real people?"

"A pawnbroker by the name of Linus Pickering."

"How did you meet?"

"I tried to bargain with him over the price of a used typewriter. I asked if he'd consider my military service as an incentive. He said all we servicemen were spoiled and didn't deserve any consideration just because we didn't go to jail for dodging the draft."

This time there was definitely a murmur, and a rustling as sitting positions changed.

"And what was your reaction?"

"I'm ashamed to say I took out my service pistol."

Absolute silence.

"You threatened him?"

"I did not. I laid it on the counter and offered him ten dollars for the typewriter."

"Mr. Heppleman, what you are describing is attempted armed robbery. The ten dollars is immaterial."

Ter Horst covered Jacob's microphone. "Don't argue."

"I never intended to take the machine at gunpoint. I said something like, 'Just for that, ten, you son of a bitch.' I was angry, not just for myself but for all the men who fought in the war, and I wanted him to know it."

"What happened then?"

"He pulled a revolver on me and I left."

St. John started to say something. Congressman Wellborn interrupted her. "Good God, Heppleman. You're beginning to sound like one of your novels."

"I'm sorry, Congressman. Is that a question?"

"No." He sat back, crossing his arms.

St. John said, "Was that the end of the affair?"

There was a pitcher of water and a glass in front of Jacob. He poured the glass half full and drank. Then he set it down and leaned forward until his lips almost touched the microphone.

"No. Hours later, after I'd had too much to drink in a bar, I came back to the shop, smashed the window with a brick, grabbed the typewriter, and ran away."

The room got noisy. A flashbulb popped; he felt the warmth on his cheek from several yards away. St. John worked her gavel until things quieted. She glared at Jacob with the stern expression of a disappointed parent.

Or maybe it was just disappointment.

"You were angry. You were drunk. Do you think that justifies your behavior?"

He said it did not, and that he regretted his actions for months. Then he told of his later meeting with Pickering and the agreement they made.

Her eyes flicked over the tops of her glasses, toward the door communicating to the waiting room. He knew now the pawnbroker would not be interviewed.

For the better part of a minute, Margery St. John paged through the sheets in a folder spread open before her. She drummed them together, removed her reading glasses, and looked at the witness.

"Mr. Heppleman, are you familiar with a man named Rodney Tharp?"

The name meant nothing at first. Seeing his blank expression, she looked down at the top sheet. "He taught an adult creative writing course in Public School 187 in New York City. You took the course in the fall of 1946."

"I remember. I don't think I knew his first name was Rodney."

For some reason someone tittered.

"Do you remember the circumstances of your last meeting?"

He felt the blood slide from his face.

Ter Horst covered the microphone. "What?"

He shook his head. It was too late. The lawyer sat back, expressionless.

"He accused me of plagiarism and I slugged him."

St. John gaveled down the spectators.

"Were you guilty of plagiarism?"

"No. The only theft I've ever been guilty of is that damn type-writer."

Orville Stahl, the representative from Delaware, spoke for the first time. His salt-and-pepper beard encircled his face like an Amish farmer's. "That's your second profanity. I caution you to watch your language, sir. Children are watching at home."

Jacob made no response. His eyes remained on St. John.

"You've established a history of violent behavior," she said at last.

"Two incidents don't make a pattern, Congresswoman. I'd just come back from a war. Adjusting to peacetime—"

"I've read some of your work, *don't forget*." She emphasized the last two words. "My aides have read all of it, and chronicled each violent act that takes place. In *The Fence* alone there are—"

"Excuse me for interrupting; I don't mean to be rude. But isn't your committee's area of interest pornography?"

"In entertainment, yes."

"I don't see what violence has to do with sex."

A chuckling issued from the gallery.

St. John glared. "Are you ridiculing the purpose of this hearing?"

"Not at all. I'm just trying to find out what it is."

"I could go deeper into the report before me and enumerate the acts of a prurient nature that occur in your work; but that would take time, and we have many other people to talk to. Instead, I'll remind you that our interest is also in juvenile delinquency. You are a father, are you not?"

"I am."

"Would you allow your daughter to read your books?"

"Not until she's of age."

"And what age would that be?"

"Thirty."

She banged down the roar of laughter hard. "One more attempt at levity and this committee will find you in contempt."

"I wasn't trying to be funny. I think it's a parent's responsibility to shield his children from material meant for adults. I wouldn't let Millie read William Faulkner at her age. I'm answering your questions, Congresswoman."

"How well do you know Philip Scarpetti?"

He looked at Ter Horst, who again gave him nothing.

"I've known him for approximately five years. He used to paint covers for Blue Devil Books."

"I'm aware of that. He's sat where you're sitting, and is serving a sentence for contempt. Do you see each other socially?"

"Not lately."

"And what did you do when you met?"

"We talked."

"Is that all you do?"

"Sometimes we drank alcohol."

Ter Horst covered the microphone. "She's about to ask if you smoke marijuana. Plead the Fifth."

But she did not.

"Mr. Heppleman, have you and Philip Scarpetti ever engaged in unnatural sexual relations?"

CHAPTER
THIRTY-EIGHT

Jacob shook his head. "Who'd have thought being a fairy is worse than being a thief?"

"Cheer up." Gilbert Ter Horst was a poster boy for chronic optimism. They sat with Ellen in a red vinyl-upholstered booth in a bar called the Veto Lounge in Chevy Chase. The waitresses wore net stockings and heels, and Tony Bennett sang from invisible speakers. The place was nearly full as dusk piled up outside and everyone seemed to be starting to have a good time. The attorney drank a vodka martini with a twist, Jacob Scotch on the rocks. A glass of Chablis stood virtually untouched in front of Ellen.

"They're done with you," the lawyer went on. "You didn't rise to their bait. You said a simple 'No' to the question St. John had been sitting on like a hen, and she couldn't get rid of you fast enough. She made a common mistake, thinking homosexuals only know other homosexuals."

"How come she believed me?"

"She expected you to blow your top; it's the oldest courtroom trick in the book. Indignation is a smoke screen for the guilty. But you couldn't be shaken. In TV parlance, you skewed honest. Don't think those camera hogs aren't wise to that."

"You thought she was going to ask if we smoked marijuana."

"That was a miscalculation, I admit. After what that prig from Delaware said about profanity, I thought they'd steer clear of calling you a fag. Well, it all came out better than I expected, and after your little confession I wouldn't be surprised if your sales figures double. Readers will think you write from experience."

"Who gives a shit? I helped Uncle Sam heap dirt on Phil's grave."

Ellen said, "Stop beating yourself up, Jake. All you could do was tell the truth."

"What's going to happen to him in Atlanta?"

"He's in isolation; standard procedure." The lawyer sipped from his funnel glass. "He'll do six months tops, and the feds take better care of inmates than anywhere else in the penal system. He'll probably put on weight."

"But how will he eat when he gets out?"

"He'll find work. He isn't the first queer to make his living with a brush."

"Jakey! Don't!" She grabbed his arm.

He let go of Ter Horst's lapels. His Scotch had dumped over. Lozenges of half-melted ice wallowed in a puddle dripping off the edge of the table. Heads turned their way.

The lawyer straightened his jacket. "I'm glad you saved that for here."

Jacob slid out of his seat, scooped money from his wallet, and laid it on a dry patch of table. "I'm sorry," he said. "You know where I am if you want to sue."

The House Select Committee on Pornography and Juvenile Delinquency adjourned at the end of its session in September 1953, with a recommendation that the paperback book industry police itself or face pressure from government. Gilbert Ter Horst called it a strategic withdrawal. Those committee members who were up for re-election returned to their home states to campaign, including Margery St. John, who beat her Republican challenger with fifty-three percent of the vote.

Jacob said, "She's going to be the first woman president."

"That or a lady wrestler," said Ellen.

"So what's the verdict?" he asked Robin Elk.

"Verdict?" The publisher, sporting a fresh London pallor, sat in the leather-upholstered conversation area in his office playing with a new cane with Queen Elizabeth II's crowned head on top in silver, a Coronation souvenir.

"The Great Cleanup. Where do we stand?"

"Almost precisely where we stood at the beginning. Congress can't tamper with the First Amendment, but just to mollify the country preachers and the PTA, the industry is toning down its covers: more clothes on the women, less blood on the floor. That's all the blighters really cared about, sensational images they could show on the news. The books' contents remain unchanged."

"What's Blue Devil doing?"

"No more paintings. We're using a pen-and-ink drawing on *The Lazy Profession*. Splendid title, by the way."

"Thanks. I was sure you'd shoot it down." He was coldly professional with Elk. Had the hearings gone a different direction, the publisher would have dropped him as fast as he had his star artist.

Elk was unmoved by his demeanor. "Who but Jack Holly would suggest that most criminals choose their path simply because they're indolent?"

"Phil Scarpetti, that's who. He was my tutor." He'd sent Scarpetti a letter in care of the federal penitentiary in Atlanta. It hadn't been returned, but there had been no reply. He'd be released soon. "So the Philistines won after all."

"It's a concession, but hardly dishonorable. The comic-book publishers have agreed to censor themselves. Television will follow suit. *Lash Logan, Private Eye* wouldn't get past the front door today, much less onto the air."

"What's Stratton up to?"

"Vanished without a trace. I've heard rumors about Korea and Tijuana. I regard Tijuana as more likely."

"The worse his luck gets, the better I like him." Jacob drank coffee. He hadn't had a drop of liquor since that day in the Veto Lounge. "Won't pen-and-ink look cheap?"

"Nothing like. We snatched this young man away from the *Saturday Evening Post*. Early sketches promise a dramatic effect, without a suggestion of sadism. Technically it's perfect." He sighed.

"What's wrong with perfect?"

"One misses the exaggerated proportions, the bright colors, the suggestion of life in the raw; the crudity, I suppose. It spoke to the belly, not the brain. The cover for *The Lazy Profession* could hang in a gallery, where anyone with the price of admission can look at it."

"Anyone always could. It cost two bits."

"As a customer, I wouldn't pay a dime a dozen for this lot. Instead I'm paying twice what I paid Scarpetti at his height. The artists have formed a union."

"I heard they're going to photographic covers at Belvedere, to get around it."

"A mistake. It will confuse readers into thinking they're buying a work of nonfiction." He leaned the cane against his chair. "I forgot to congratulate you. Winderspear informs me Edvard Kaspar's going ahead with *The Fence*."

"Filming's started. The Breen Office made him change the title, to separate it from all the controversy. He's shooting it under *Stolen Goods*. But it may change again."

"How do you feel about that?"

"It stinks, but I don't care. I just put twenty thousand in the bank."

Elk's chipmunk eyes brightened. "Now that you're in the black I don't suppose I can interest you in a new contract."

"I'm not touching the Hollywood money. It's going into Millie's college fund."

"We can talk, then."

"No dice, Robin. I've had an offer from Dunlap for two books, sight unseen. They saw my manly profile on TV and think it'll look good on the jacket flap. There was never any room for it on the back of a Blue Devil book, among all those exclamation points."

"Hardcover's a step down, not up. You get a hundred percent of the royalties now. Dunlap will sell subsidiary rights to a paperback house—mine, possibly—and take half."

The man was all greed; worse than Irish Mickey Shannon in his way. Mickey at least had the virtue of personal pride. His old push for a piece of the action was symbolic; a balm for his hard-won criminal wisdom suddenly offered cheap for the masses. It would continue to fester no matter how many years he spent in an eight-by-ten cell. There was nothing symbolic about Robin Elk's avarice.

"It will be a nice change to see a customer laying my book faceup on the counter of a real bookstore."

"That will happen regardless. Someday the world will catch up with you jaded fellows and realize you were the ones telling the truth all along. You'll get the respect you deserve without compromising your principles."

Jacob laughed. "Elk, you wouldn't recognize a principle if it walked up and kicked that cane out from under you."

PART FIVE

1978

HUNDRED BUCKS A PLATE

CHAPTER
THIRTY-NINE

The room was cavernous, dwarfing the crowd, packed so tightly the people could only shuffle forward as they entered. Signs and banners identified the booths, and barn door–size blowups of movie posters and book covers made startling splashes of color: The scarlet lips of the slinky temptress on *Chinese Checkers* were as big as a sofa.

"Mr. Holly?"

"Heppleman." He shook the young man's hand.

"I'm Earl Frame. We spoke on the phone."

Frame wore a sportcoat over a T-shirt and blue jeans.

"My daughter, Mildred."

He colored before the tall redhead at Jacob's side. She took his hand, smiling. "Hello."

"Hello. Um, has anyone ever told you that you look like the woman on the original cover of *The Fence*?"

"No, but I'm told I resemble my mother."

He cleared his throat. "Mr. Heppleman, you're scheduled to sign at two, after you deliver the keynote. That's when the interest is highest. Is that all right?"

Jacob had leaned in to hear him. "I don't guess it matters. I'm not Erica Jong. In the old days, we didn't bother with signings. Back then people read paperbacks and threw them away or passed them on. No one collected them."

"Times have changed. I'll show you where you're speaking."

The banquet hall was nearly as large as the exhibition room. Waiters were setting out dishes and flatware on round linen-covered tables, with numbers clipped to stands in the centers and eight chairs to each. A wooden lectern stood on a riser at the far end. On the wall behind it hung a swallowtail-shaped banner with a dozen of Jack Holly's covers reproduced on it in full color.

"Amazing," he said. "And in broad daylight. But I'll never fill the joint."

"We're sold out, at a hundred dollars a plate."

He touched the gizmo in his ear. There must have been some distortion.

Millie patted his arm. "You're too modest, Dad. Mom would've been so proud."

"She was proud of me regardless. Her one blind spot."

She'd had two, actually, counting cigarettes. *Don't be sad, Jakey. I had the time of my life.*

Frame interrupted his thoughts. "The fund's intended to provide aid to struggling writers and graphic artists."

"Where was it when I needed it?"

"We're really delighted you could make it, sir. There aren't many of your colleagues in condition to attend. Phoebe Sternwalter died while we were in correspondence. Burt Woods and Paul Arthur won't share the same building; they write on opposite coasts and mail pages to each other. We offered to fly Robin Elk from the U.K. at our expense, but he declined through a secretary."

"I heard he became a recluse after he sold his father's firm."

"The artists are a special challenge. Phil Scarpetti's old address is no good. He did all your covers, didn't he?"

"Most of them, yes."

He'd spotted Phil five years ago on the subway, or thought he had. He'd aged badly; but who'd ever had practice at that? He was in the company of a young man. He met Jacob's gaze, briefly and without sign of recognition. The pair got off at the next stop. For Jacob it was like reading the obituary of someone he'd once been close to.

Back in the exhibition room, a woman passed wearing a skin-tight gold lamé jumpsuit with brass-embossed breasts. He remembered the series. *Glamazons,* by Hugh Brock.

Brock's wife woke up one morning while he was pouring gasoline on a pile of her clothes in the bedroom. He'd died in Bellevue.

Someone spoke. He started. "What?"

"You'll have to speak up," Millie said. "My father's a little hard of hearing."

Earl Frame raised his voice. "You knew Cliff Cutter, didn't you?"

"Not well; but I admired him."

"I think you'll appreciate this." The young man walked away briskly.

Millie said, "I guess we're supposed to follow him."

"I should've brought a bicycle."

They stopped at a booth at the end of a long aisle, where a crowd was dispersing. A stout old woman busied herself arranging items in a sort of museum display. Panels of weathered barnwood had been erected to form a room within the room. A Winchester carbine, an ivory-handled Colt in a worn holster, lariats, coppertone photos of Indian braves shared the space with a rolltop desk and a battered old Underwood typewriter. Cutter might have just stepped out of the rustic study for a breath of desert air.

"We trucked it all in directly from his place in Denver," Frame said. "Everything's just as he left it. He wrote most of his westerns in that room. It's the most popular booth in the exhibition."

"Jack?"

He stared at the old woman. "Nayoka?" It was Cliff Cutter's Navajo wife. He recognized the bright black eyes, sunk deep in folds of fat. He took her hand gently.

She beamed first at him, then at Millie. "How old are you, child?"

The question surprised her into laughter. "I'll be thirty next March."

Nayoka turned back to Jacob. "I told you. Indian medicine is still strong."

"We put that carving in a safe-deposit box when Millie was teething." He changed the subject. "This is an impressive display. I can feel his presence."

"He'd be furious. They put everything in wrong. He wouldn't let me in even to clean. You know how he died."

"I heard it was a stroke."

"That happened in the hospital after they set his hip. He fell off his horse galloping down a ravine: showing off for his young ranch hands. He was ninety-two."

Earl Frame introduced him to a hall filled to capacity. He'd expected wheelchairs and trifocals, and there were some of those among the white heads, but younger people as well. A little girl in the front row reminded him of Millie when she was ten. He'd raised her alone.

He started strong.

"Um."

A shrill electronic whistle made many in the audience clap their hands over their ears. He'd leaned in too close.

"Forgive me," he said, increasing the distance. "The last time I spoke into a microphone, I was in a Congressional hearing room."

This brought laughter. It was a savvy crowd.

His remarks were brief. He gave thanks for the invitation and warm reception and told anecdotes about the writing life. After prolonged applause, Frame stepped up to encourage questions.

Most were routine: where he got his ideas, his working method, his opinion of the movies based on his books. One he mulled over. It was asked by a young woman in a business suit with a floppy bow tie. "Mr. Holly—"

"Heppleman, please."

"I'm sorry. Under what authority did the United States Congress claim the right to censor the literature?"

He paused, then: "The times were different. The Coast Guard confiscated French novels at the docks. Comic books were burned publicly in church parking lots. Juvenile delinquency was a crisis, and some well-meaning people thought they could eradicate it at the source—if they could just identify the source.

"It was nothing new. When I was a boy, it was radio: *Gangbusters* and Jack Benny were raising a generation of illiterates. Later it was television. Now it's video arcades. The difference is more people are paying lip service to the First Amendment. Not that it amounts to any more than that, but back then such talk branded you a Communist."

He finished to a standing ovation.

On his way to the booth where he was to sign, a middle aged man in a denim jacket and jeans approached him. "Mr. Heppleman, I'm Kurt Krohner. I'm with the *Post*." He showed a press card. "Can I ask you some things?"

"If you don't mind walking with me."

Krohner trotted alongside. "Your kind of book is getting a great deal more respect these days."

"Any amount would be more than we got."

"Why the change?"

"The world caught up."

"I'm sorry?"

He stopped walking and faced the reporter.

"Many of us were just back from the war. You can't see cities being bombed, corpses piled in concentration camps, and dish out happy endings. We wrote about a world that had changed, and we pointed out where it took a wrong turn. For that we were called smut peddlers. Then along came political scandals, pointless wars, and men's peckers on movie screens where Shirley Temple used to sing and dance. It took all that for everyone else to see what we saw. So now we're serious artists who weren't afraid to tell it like it was."

He was paraphrasing Robin Elk, he knew. It didn't change his opinion of the man. He resumed walking.

"Is that how you saw yourselves?" Krohner scrambled to catch up.

"Hell, no. We wanted to put away enough dough so we could get out of the paperback jungle and write respectable."

Krohner scribbled as they walked. They detoured around a line that snaked around several booths in the dealers' room. The customers obscured whoever it was signing behind the table. Jacob said, "Who's that, do you know?"

The reporter traded his notebook for a folded program. "That private-eye guy, Stratton. I'd say he's in demand."

Officially Jacob was there to sign *The Valley Forge Murders,* his latest revolutionary historical mystery, and Dunlap had provided two hundred copies. But the old Blue Devil titles had been reissued in paper by Lighthouse Books, and they outsold the hardcover ten to one. Earl Frame stood beside the table, opening the books for him to inscribe, with Millie present to hand them to each person in line; a factory operation that rarely obliged Jacob to look up into the faces.

"You write all these books yourself?"

He looked up then.

Hank Stratton's grin was stuck to a slack face, his formerly steely eyes bloodshot now and settled deep in their sockets. He'd exchanged his trademark fedora and trench coat for a Yankees cap and powder-blue leisure suit.

They shook hands. The P. I. writer's grip was as firm as always. He snatched the Lighthouse edition of *The Fence* off the top of the stack and handed it to Jacob. "I never did get past the first couple of chapters; lost my copy during a move."

He inscribed it to Stratton—that made it an association copy, one author to another—and gave it back. A tall blonde in a tight red dress had appeared at Stratton's side. "You promised me a drink," she said.

He leered at Jacob. "Meet my nurse."

After the pair left, Millie said, "I remember you telling me about him. He sure landed on his feet."

"And to think I almost liked him once."

———

Jacob sold out. When the last purchaser drifted off, he stood and stretched. His right leg had gone to sleep.

"Ready to go, Dad?" Millie twined her arm inside his.

"While I still have stars in my eyes."

An elevator took them down to an underground parking garage. It was lit by bulbs in cages and smelled of oil and engine exhaust and damp; a scene from a Holly novel.

"Wait here, Dad. I'll bring the car around."

He watched her walk away down the aisle. His eyes lost focus. Through them he saw her mother's careless stride.

"Jack Holly!"

He swung toward the deep coarse voice.

A stunted dark figure was coming his way from the shadowy end of the garage, a broad-tailed coat spreading behind it, a hat with a dimpled crown on its head. Steel taps clicked on concrete.

The figure came into focus. Time had closed its fist on that face, crumpling it into thousands of creases.

"Mickey?"

"Irish Mickey died in the joint," said the dwarf. "Nobody's called me that since I got out. I'm Izzy Muntz again. This is for you." He stuck a hand inside his shabby coat. The Luger was gone, probably in police custody long since; the short stubby revolver was more to his scale.

Jacob threw out his hands, as if he could catch the bullet between them, like a moth.

Sudden bright light threw his shadow across the little man's face. Jacob was already moving, out of the line of fire. The car sped past him, close enough to lift his coat, its headlamps drenching the gunman in blinding white. Shannon's face was a rictus of shock.

Steel slammed into flesh, a ghastly noise. His feet left the floor, his body flying up and over the hood. He might have been diving to meet the threat. Brakes shrieked. Then he was airborne. His body hung at the top of the arc, just under the low ceiling, for an impossible length of time, then came down on its back with a sickening wet smack.

"Dad!" Millie was out of the car, the door hanging open. The hood was crumpled up against the windshield. She caught her father in her arms as he lost his balance. She shivered in his embrace.

"Are you all right?" He was shouting.

"That man! He—"

"He's sick!" He shook her by the shoulders. "Are you all right?"

She bobbed her head up and down. Her teeth were chattering.

More footsteps clattered. A security guard in a gray uniform was running their way, unbuttoning his holster as he came. He stopped before the tiny figure lying broken at his feet, spreading his arms to hold back a crowd appearing as from empty air.

Jacob squeezed Millie's arms, patted them; a lame attempt at reassurance. He disengaged himself with effort—she was holding him in a death grip—made sure she could stand on her own, then stepped forward to kneel beside Irish Mickey Shannon.

The dwarf was a sack of shattered bone. A gray mist came through his prison pallor. He was wheezing. Blood spilled from his nostrils and over his chin. On an impulse, Jacob took off his coat, lifted the dying man's head gently, and doubled the coat over to make a pillow.

"You should've gone straight, Mickey," he heard himself saying. "We might have collaborated on your memoirs. You'd have been upstairs, signing autographs next to me. Getting respect."

Shannon's eyes had lost their gloss, but teeth gleamed through the blood in a grotesque grin. Jacob had to lean close, turning his better ear to hear what the little man was saying before it ended in a rattle.

"Respect," he said. "Where's the fun in that?"

Recommended Reading

A slew of research went into the writing of *Paperback Jack*. The following sources were among the most valuable:

Gruber, Frank. *The Pulp Jungle.* Los Angeles: Sherbourne Press, 1967. Gruber comes off as a cheat, a bully, and a sore loser; but hack that he was, his experiences writing for the pulp market in its declining years cast a strong light on a nearly forgotten culture.

O'Brien, Geoffrey. *Hardboiled America: The Lurid Years of Paperbacks.* New York: Van Nostrand Reinhold, 1981. This 144-page hardcover is a compact delight, for its comprehensive history of the paperback revolution, excerpts from transcripts from the hearings held in 1952 by the House Select Committee on Current Pornographic Materials (the model for the House Select Committee on Pornography and Juvenile Delinquency), and sixteen scrumptious pages of full-color reproductions of lurid paperback covers. The artists, anonymous in their time, receive proper recognition here.

Server, Lee. *Danger Is My Business: An Illustrated History of the Fabulous Pulp Magazines: 1896–1953.* San Francisco: Chronicle Books, 1993. Server, well-known for his classic movie-star biographies, provides us with a coffee table–size trade paperback stuffed with color illustrations of covers and a straightforward narrative of the history of the pulp magazine industry from Buffalo Bill to Ray Bradbury. A handy appendix helps guide the reader through the world of pulp collecting.

Server, Lee. *Over My Dead Body: The Sensational Age of the American Paperback: 1945–1955*. San Francisco: Chronicle Books, 1994. This companion volume to *Danger Is My Business* gives the same full Server treatment to the territory previously covered by Geoffrey O'Brien. Once again, he "serves up" stunning four-color covers, names for the nameless, and details on the development of modern American literature.

Finally, I cannot recommend too strenuously the original works of Leigh Brackett, Harlan Ellison, David Goodis, Donald Hamilton, Chester Himes, John D. MacDonald, Richard Matheson, Horace McCoy, William P. McGivern, Les Savage, Jr., Gordon D. Shirreffs, and Jim Thompson; and of as many of their fellow pioneers who await your discovery. You will find many of them in garage sales, used bookstores, and in new editions released by respected publishers—including the prestigious Library of America.